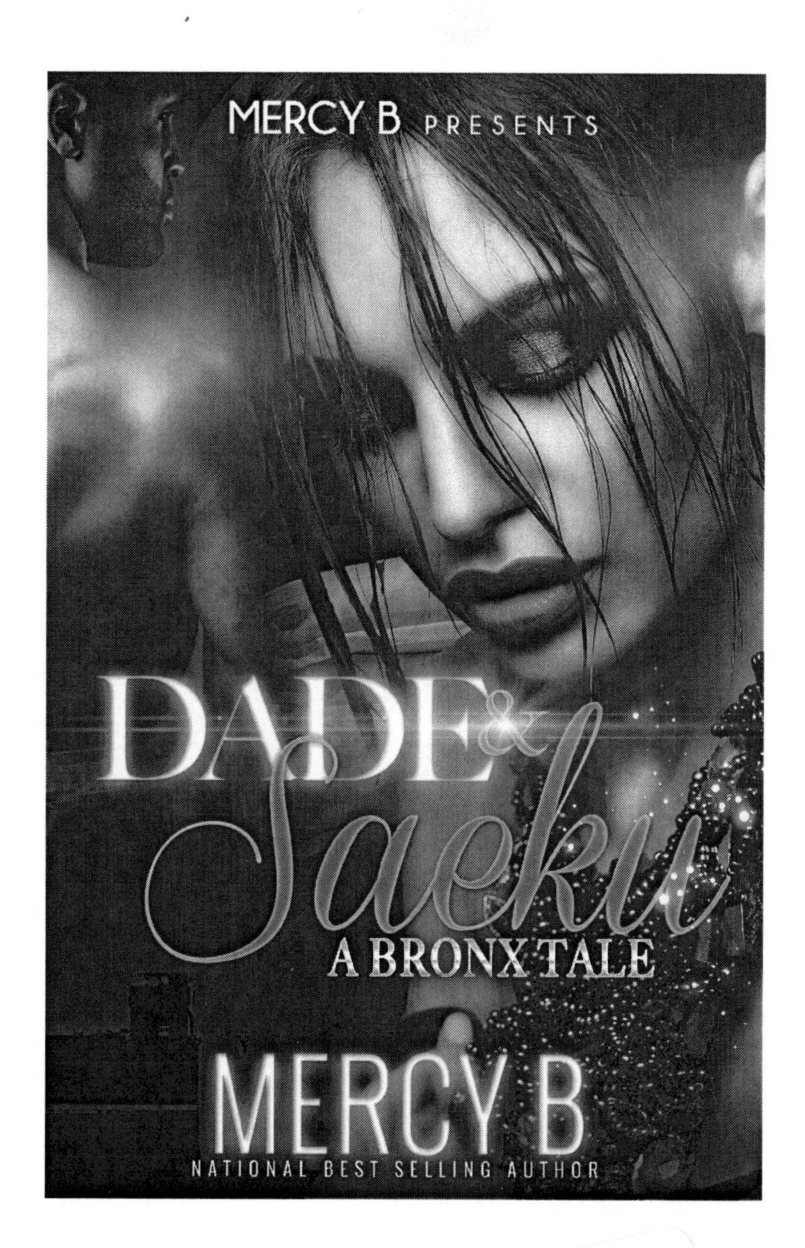
MERCY B PRESENTS
DADE & Saeku
A BRONX TALE
MERCY B
NATIONAL BEST SELLING AUTHOR

D0967953

Dade & A Bronx SaeKu Tale

by National Bestselling Author Mercy B

Published by Mercy B Publications

Dedication

To the girl who has struggled with forgiveness in life and in love.

-Mercy

Acknowledgements

We've got us another one, God. Hats off!

To everyone who's supported my journey, thank you!

Please Note That This Is A Spin-Off.

List of Books Including SaeKu & Dade:

RahMeek & Bella 1-5: A Philly Love Story

Youngin' Blues: The Story of Reed and RaKeem

Secrecy: The Story of KinZu Noble

Dade & SaeKu: A Bronx Tale

by National Bestselling Author Mercy B

The Prologue...

Phst. Phst.

Dade cleared the thick globs of mucus from his mouth. Rolling his tongue across his teeth, he stared down at the thick patch of dirt that covered the single individual that had caused havoc in his life, his mother. As much as he hated her, he could never stray far from her corpse. He figured it was his way of making sure that she was still there, still amongst the dead –unable to ruin his life any more than she already had.

The clouds emptied their loads, sprinkling fine bits of water onto his trench, signaling his timely departure. However, he was frozen into place. Like every other time that he visited his mother's grave, he couldn't bring himself to pick up his feet to leave. As any child would, young or old, he'd wanted these moments to be filled with joy and memorable moments, but all Dade felt was resentment and pain.

A million questions lingered in his head as he stared down at the beautiful headstone that he'd supplied her with. Attempting at a piece of normalcy, he figured that it was the least that he could do –being that she did birth and bring him life. Besides, Dade needed something worth while to lay his eyes upon, knowing that so much time would be spent gazing at the grey stone.

"Babe," Dade felt a small hand on the lower half of his back.

Turning around, he pulled Alani into his side, and kissed her forehead. "What's up?" he questioned.

"Our flight leaves soon, and we need to get home to pack."

"You're right." Dade sighed.

He insisted on Alani staying behind for the ride, but she insisted on accompanying him. Knowing that no one could truly understood the complexity of his visits, he was attempting to be considerate. After the back and forth, he ended up bringing her along anyway.

Placing the single black rose in the small metal holder, Dade lifted himself and grabbed Alani's hand. Together, they walked to the midnight blue Range Rover before, both, getting inside. Leaning back in his seat, Dade took a deep breath, and massaged his temple. It bothered him more than anyone would ever fathom to not be able to celebrate the legacy of his mother, and have wonderful memories flood his mental as he visited.

Within seconds, Dade gathered himself, and started the truck. Visits to the grave were mentally and emotionally exhausting. His childhood was a very sore subject, and the remembrance of if was forever altered during times as such. Neglect heavy on his heart, Dade tried to lift the temporary burden by thinking of his plans for the next week. A much needed vacation was in the works. For once, he wanted to relax, and not consider that piles of shit that he had going on back home.

"Shit. We have thirty minutes." Dade was pissed, because they'd wasted time getting more familiar with each other's body parts, as if they didn't know enough about them enough. Their hour to pack turned into two. Now, they were both paying for it big time.

Dade checked his watch as they made their way into the airport. His rain coat had been exchanged for a black hoodie. The New York weather was rather nice, so it was no longer necessary. Besides, the rain had subsided as they journeyed from the cemetery to their home. Alani was dressed in a pair of jeans and a tee. Her simple attire was very chic, but classy. She flowed through the airport, effortlessly.

"Let's just pray that we make it." Alani crossed her fingers, and said a quick prayer.

"Take your shoes off." Dade begin hopping, trying to get his left shoe off.

"Huh?" Alani looked down at him as if he was crazy.

"Take your shoes off." Dade said, again. "We can skip that line if we're prepared. You have the boarding passes, right?"

"Yeah. They're right here." Alani assured him, pulling the passes from her purse.

As the two sped through the airport, they removed their shoes. When they were finally upon TSA, they bypassed the bulk and was directed to priority checking. Dade was relieved that they'd been able to get through, quickly. Now, they needed to find their gate before their plane departed.

Never again. He kicked his own ass for scheduling a private flight near the time of their departure. Had he listened to his homies, then he wouldn't have had to step foot inside of an airport. That shit was for the birds. The crew had flown over the seas, together. They'd fired up the jet, and took off. As collected as Dade was, he was about ready to lose his cool. He hated rushing, and dealing with crowds of people all moving at once.

He had the right mind to drive to Philly that morning, but he was busy tying up lose ends. Besides, they hadn't packed one thing. It wasn't like him to lose a grip on time, but so much shit had happened in the last three days that he hadn't had much time to do anything. He made a mental note to call his aunt once he landed, because she was going to chew him a new asshole for not checking in with her before he left. That was his heart and soul, but she could be the meanest woman in the world when she wanted to be.

The normal hustle and bustle of the airport made Dade's head spin, and anxiety to reach its maximum potential. What was even worse was the fact that they were running behind. He refused to miss his flight, so he put a little pep in his step.

"Come on." He pulled Alani's arm, and forced her to shuffle her feet a bit faster. Their suitcases were small, being that they'd packed light. With both being the size of carry-ons, neither of them had to check them.

"This is us!" Alani yelled out as they made it to their gate.

Just as Dade thought, they were calling for first class. That was their cue. Alani handed the reps their boarding passes, and the two was cleared to get on the plane. After tucking their bags in the overhead compartment, Dade took a seat beside Alani.

As the rest of the passengers boarded, Dade reclined his seat, and pulled out his headphones. "You good?" he asked Alani before plugging them into his ears, and pulling his hoodie tight around his face.

"Yeah. I'm fine, baby."

"I'm going to get some shut eye. Wake me when we land."

"Okay." Alani watched as the passengers took their seats and got comfortable. Within 20 minutes, the Captain was announcing take-off.

Besides the cooing sounds of the baby a few rows back from Dade and Alani, the plane was silent. The small screens dispensed from the overheads, and the plane policies and emergency procedures begin to play. For two minutes, everyone on board was forced to hear the redundant sounds of a prerecorded video ahead.

"We've reached 34,000 feet. The skies have cleared, so it looks like we're going to have a smooth flight. Our attendants are going to be sweeping through the aisles with complimentary drinks and snacks. Thanks for flying with us, folks." The captain ended his announcement as the carts begin to make their way down the aisle. Starting with first class, the attendants offered water, apple juice, and crackers to each passenger of the flight.

As the Flight attendant neared Alani, she admired the beautiful waves that she'd had professionally done just before the flight. She wanted to ask about them, but women were always weird about sharing their beauty secrets, so Alani decided against it.

"Would you like anything to snack on or drink?" the attendant asked.

"Yes. This little girl has me starving." Alani rubbed her round stomach, causing a smile to tug at the attendant's lips.

"What would you like? Water, apple ju…"

"Apple juice, and some of the crackers that you have in your hand."

"Here. How about two packs, for you and the little one."

"Thanks. Baby…" Alani turned and began to shake Dade. He'd tilted over on the window in order to get a little more comfortable. "He may want something." Alani continued to shake Dade until he lifted up, and turned her way. His earbuds fell from his ears, as he faced her.

"You want anything?" Alani questioned.

"Uh. Yeah. Apple juice…"

"Apple jui…" This time, SaeKu's words were cut short. Seemingly, her airways had been restricted all of a sudden. Staring back at Dade, she tried to gather her thoughts and move her feet along, but she was stuck in place. His face was still as handsome as the last time she'd seen him. The sympathy displayed in his eyes caused a fury fire to burn in SaeKu's chest.

"Apple juice." Alani finished her sentence. "We will both have apple juice."

"Yes. Right. Apple juice." SaeKu bent down, and grabbed two cups. Her hands were unsteady and shaky as she poured the two cups of apple juice before handing them to Alani.

With sweaty palms, she pushed her cart to the back of the plane, not minding the passengers who were beckoning for her attention. She didn't give a shit if they never ate or drunk a sip during the flight. If it was up to her to serve them, then they'd all starve to death.

"Sage." SaeKu called out to her best friend.

"What's up?" Sage was stationed near the back, so she was able to get to her in a split second.

"He's here."

"Who's here?"

"Dade!" SaeKu cut her eyes toward the front of the plane.

"Let me see." Sage gave SaeKu a once over. "You look good. Your waves are popping. Make up on fleek. Teeth white… Edges presence… Baby hair laying… What's with the puppy face? You've waited for this day."

Sage and SaeKu were polar opposites. Sage was fair skinned with the most beautiful set of big round eyes. While SaeKu's skin was dark and rich in melanin, Sage's color told stories of her family history. Although she considered herself black, there were traces of Caucasian in her complexion. SaeKu's was thin, while Sage's hips and ass stuck out like sore thumbs. SaeKu was the more reserved friend, but Sage was outspoken by nature. They were a perfect match, and years had brought them closer and closer.

"That's just it."

"What?"

"It's nothing like I imagined. He's with someone."

"Awwww shit." Sage covered her mouth after a slip of the tongue. She could feel her girl's pain.

Dade's mind was racing a mile a minute as he thought of the odds of him seeing SaeKu at such a compromising time. Looking over at Alani, he wished he could close his eyes, open them again, and her presence would have magically disappeared. Even though it was wishful thinking, he tried, anyway. Unfortunately, he opened his eyes to Alani stuffing another cracker into her mouth.

"Damn." He shook his head.

"Huh?" Alani turned with a questioning look.

"Nothing." He responded, taking a peek towards the back of the plane. "Shit."

"Huh?" Alani knew she wasn't crazy.

"Nothing. Let me get through." Dade unbuckled his seatbelt and climbed out of the tight space. "I need to use the restroom."

Dade's long frame traveled the length of the plane until he reached the area he'd witnessed SaeKu disappear into. "Excuse me sir. You can't…" Sage begin, but quieted once Dade started to speak to SaeKu. Passengers weren't allowed in the restricted area, but she'd allow it under the circumstances.

"SaeKu." He started.

That was Sage's cue to leave. She pulled the curtain back as she left the area, promising SaeKu that she would cover first class for her. SaeKu thanked her, and waited before speaking again.

"Dade." SaeKu hung her head.

"Straighten your face." Dade's demanded. "Let me explain."

"No need to explain."

"Here we go." He chuckled. "SaeKu, has nothing changed?"

"Dade. Really. Just go back up there."

"Answer the question."

"Obviously, a whole fucking lot has changed."

"Look, I'm sorry."

"Right."

"What else am I supposed to say?"

"Nothin." SaeKu shrugged. "It's nice seeing you."

"Can I get a number on you or something?" Dade asked.

"Dade, let's not go there."

"Do you get a kick out of shutting me out or some shit? Does that get you off?"

"Dade. I could lose my job with you being back here. Please. Just go back up there."

"Fuck this job, SaeKu. I could have you flying with the elite before they could even blink."

"Thanks, but I happen to love where I am."

Both Dade and SaeKu were silent, staring into one another's eyes. So much was said in the short amount of time, and not one word was used to say it. Every thought and emotion caused by the emptiness that they both shared from one another's absence was spoken for. Each lonely night that the other had wished they were near being remembered. Everything. In that moment, everything was acknowledged.

"I think about you so fucking much." Dade admitted.

"Dade. Just please." SaeKu dropped her head, and placed it in her hand. She contained her composure as silence swept over their space once more.

"SaeKu." He reached out for her, but she moved from within his reach.

"Just please… Go." She held her hand up with the meanest scowl on her face. She was hurting, and his voice was doing nothing for the pain.

Feeling defeated, Dade granted her wish, and removed himself from her presence. SaeKu kept her head down as he walked towards his newly found happiness, ripping a piece of her once whole heart with each step he took down the narrow aisle. SaeKu knew at that moment that the life she was merely getting on track had derailed, promising tragedy.

Chapter One

"Dear Lord, I ask that you continue on your way. I won't ask you of nothing but a few things. Bless my mother," squeezing his mother's hand, Lorde slightly opened his eyes and witnessed his mother's faint smile. Bowing his head, he continued to pray. "Keep her in good health. Lord, you've been her strength for the last year, and I ask that you continue to be so. Besides that, I ask that you protect a nigga out here in these streets, because I may not always be able to get to my heat."

"LORDE!" his mother drew her hand back and stared at him through chastising eyes.

"What mama? You asked me to pray, and this is how I talk to God. Homie understands. You pray your way and I pray mine." Lorde shrugged his shoulders. "Now, bow your head, because I've got to get out of here."

"I don't know what I'm going to do with you, boy." Lauren bowed her head as her son continued to pray.

"Like I was saying, protect me when I'm without the strap. Strip all of these fake niggas and thirsty tricks from my vicinity. Rid me of anyone who's not of good service to my empire. Guide me as I rest on my throne. Keep leadership over my life. Lord, I also want to thank you for my health and my livelihood. Mama nearly had a heart attack when I handed her them keys, but once again, you saved her." Lorde chuckled. Lauren lifted her hand and swatted his back. "Sorry," he winced, "but that's about it for now. Amen."

"What?" Lorde grabbed his mother's face and kissed her aging skin.

Day by day, her health was failing her a little bit more. Cancer was eating away at her bones, but she was still hanging in. The doctors had given her six months to live after diagnosing her with stage five bone cancer, but that was a year ago. Luckily, she was still breathing to date.

"Nothing, boy. Who told you that that's the way you pray to God?"

"Mama, I read my bible. That man," Lorde pointed towards the ceiling, "Can call bullshit a mile away. For that reason alone, I make sure that I come to him solid. 100. It's the only way I know how to be. Shit, you taught me that."

"I also taught you not to use so much damn profanity." Lauren pinched Lorde's arm, making him squeal.

"And look at you?" Lorde burst into laughter, rubbing the patch that burned from the pinch.

"Let me help you back in bed, and get out of here." Lorde insisted.

He had a few plays to make, and needed to be gone like yesterday. However, it was he and his mother's thing to pray, so he wouldn't miss that for the world. Tonight, she had a change of plans and had him to do the honors.

"Where is Dade? I haven't heard from him in two days. He's smelling his ass."

"He's on vacation, ma. What you expect? Him to sit on the phone with you while he's trying to relax."

"Did he take that heffa with him?"

"Alani? Yes."

"Hmph."

"Man, chill." Lorde laughed. His mother was the sweetest lady, but she played no games when it came to her boys. Dade was Lorde's cousin, but Lauren had raised him as her own.

"Has that girl had that baby, yet?"

"You mean has Gia had my daughter, Pryce, yet?"

"I've told you before, and I'll tell you again. That baby is not yours. You and Dade are around here claiming children that have nothing to do with y'all. I'd be glad when one of you give me some grandchildren, for real."

"She hasn't even made her arrival, yet. How can you just assume that?"

"I feel it. I feel in my bones. It's killing me quicker than this cancer. Seeing you walking around with a silly ass grin plastered on your face, and that girl is making a fool of you."

"Don't say that."

"Well, it's the truth, Lorde. God. How can you not see right through her shit?"

"Up. Up. Up." Lorde bent down and lifted his mother in her arms.

In the last year, she'd gotten so much thinner than she'd always been. Her weight had plummeted the minute she was diagnosed. Lorde was convinced that knowing was leading her to her death sooner than the actual disease. However, he still kept hope alive. They'd agreed to refuse the chemotherapy offered, and opted out for a healthier diet. In both of their opinions, that decision was keeping her alive longer than doctor's had predicted.

After making sure that his mother was tucked in, Lorde kissed her goodbye, and hopped in his coupe, blasting Young Jeezy's "Thug Motivation." As he cruised through the city streets, Gia and Pryce both crossed his mind.

Lorde was 100% sure that Pryce wouldn't share the same blood as him, but he was the only hope that the little girl had. Without him, she didn't stand a chance. Her mother hated the thought of birthing a child into the world, because she was so fucking selfish. After two years with her, Lorde couldn't figure out why he hadn't noticed it sooner.

Much like his mother, he was willing to care for an orphan, one who wasn't biologically his. Yet, Lorde couldn't see himself turning the cheek on the innocent baby girl. With his mother's health dwindling, it was all the more reason to give her a grandchild, and award him with someone to love unconditionally after she perished.

Gia was forever running game, assuming that she was getting over, but Lorde was smarted than most took him for. With a Masters in Mass Communications, Lorde wasn't the average dealer. His dealings were strictly professional, and only his hood persona pled his case – giving up his occupation almost on contact. Without it, no one would be able to guess that he was head of New York's largest drug operation.

Well-mannered, professional, knowledgeable, conscious, and groomed to perfection, Lorde was every woman's dream and every dealer's arch enemy. Not once had he intentionally been the center of chaos or destruction, but jealousy was amongst him. Nigga's simply hated to see the young brother get his motherfucking roll on.

Standing at a whopping 6'4 with legs for days, Lorde towered over his prey. His deep chocolate skin and set of dimples made women crumble at his feet. As if someone had prowled his legs apart, they separated, forming a noticeable parenthesis. Lauren had always emphasized the fact that he had bowed legs just as his father, but Lorde had never met the man. He died in a tragic car accident, rushing to the hospital to see his namesake enter the world.

Pearly whites adorned his handsome face, and a goatee complimented them. Unlike the average New Yorker, with a patch of hair on his head or loose dreads, Lorde's roof was as smooth as a baby's bottom. Channeling out the bass in his speakers, he pulled his cell from his pocket, and answered.

"Yo?"

"I seen her." Dade spat through the phone, barely above a whisper.

"What, nigga?"

"I seen her, yo?"

"Who?"

"SaeKu. The girl I've been telling you about."

"Are you ducked off?" Lorde asked, cackling like an animal.

"Fuck you, nigga!" Dade spit at him. "I'm serious right now, yo. I've been looking for her ass for over a year, and she finally pops up… Only at the wrong damn time. Now, she ain't going to never give me a chance. She was bugging the fuck out."

"So, you're about to spend your entire vacation caught in some sick ass love triangle. You can either send your shorty back, or hang that shit up."

"She ain't here, man."

"Well, how did you see her?"

"She's a flight attendant, and was on our flight."

"Let me guess… You let her get away, again."

"Na." Dade rubbed his hand over his face, stressed beyond relief.

SaeKu was heavy on his mind, and frankly, on his heart. The pained expression that crossed her beautiful face touched Dade more than he'd like to admit. Even after so much time had elapsed, she still had the same affect on him.

"So what you do?"

Dade watched behind him as SaeKu gathered her belongings, and prepared to exit the plane as well. The first class section had long ago cleared, but Dade and Alani had stayed behind because he'd taken much too long to get himself together once the door had opened. He was purposely stalling in order to dissect SaeKu's movements, and find out exactly what was her next move.

The navy blue luggage that she pulled behind her was a sure sign that this, too, was her exit. With her head held high, avoiding making eye contact, she pursued the cabin's exit. For a split second, he was worried but remembered that there was one more flight to catch before making it to their destination –which meant that SaeKu wouldn't be in attendance. Besides, he'd hoped that the guys would've mentioned it if she was. Alani would've been home had SaeKu's name even been hinted at.

"Uh. Go ahead." Dade nudged Alani, urging her to make her exit.

"Okay babe." She called out before stepping from their row, holding her designer bag on her right arm.

The words that spewed from her MAC polished lips caused a rippling affect in SaeKu's chest –stinging her like a bee protecting its hive. She'd reached the couple just as they were making their way out of their assigned seating. Alani's large stomach caused a light wobble in her strut, insulting SaeKu's mental with each step.

Closing her eyes, she counted to three before reopening them, and recollecting her thoughts. She tried her hardest to seem unfazed, but her tactics failed miserably as Dade sighed while staring at her perfectly chiseled face. SaeKu, a younger version of her sister, KinZu, with even more slanted eyes and structured cheeks. Her heritage shined through her features, and couldn't be hidden even if she attempted.

Starting behind Alani, Dade turned towards SaeKu with pleading eyes. If only he could have a second of her time, he would explain the situation at hand. Desperately, he wanted her to know that it was nothing that it seemed to be. Even still after so much time, she meant the entire world to him, and leaving her with a bad taste in her mouth to go along with his name would crush him.

"I have to go to the ladies' room." Alani rubbed her round stomach as they stepped into the airport. Dade barely paid her much mind as she wobbled to the restroom that was directly ahead of them. "Dade," she turned back.

"Uh. Yeah." He asked, eyes trained on SaeKu as she walked passed Alani, seemingly in a hurry. She, too, was headed to the restroom.

"Okay, I'll be right back. Just stay here. We have a two-hour layover."

"I know. Go ahead. I'll be here."

Taking the first open seat he came across, closest to the restroom, Dade made it his. His right foot bounced up and down as he surveyed his surroundings. He felt like a kid before a huge recital. Nervous was an understatement, and he couldn't understand. This girl really had him tripping out.

Although a retired illegal product pusher, he had adapted to the ways of one, and would never go astray. In a few seconds, his eyes landed back on the entrance of the women's restroom. Gazing at the hole in the wall, he watched as women continued to go in and out. The bland colored walls had him lost in a trance as he thought of the things he could say to SaeKu to make shit better.

The urge to go inside crossed his mind several times, but he didn't want to alarm the women, and be forced from the airport before their flight departed. Alani's presence suddenly meant nothing to him. He was willing to risk whatever it was that they had in order to see to SaeKu.

As his Nike Air Forces pounded against the polished tile on the floor, his heart raced. There was no way in hell was he letting SaeKu get away from him this time. He'd waited for what seemed like forever for her to reenter his life, and there she was. A true believer in fate, he knew that this had to be apart of it's work.

"FUCK IT." He called out to no one in particular.

Standing to his feet, he rubbed his jet black goatee, and chuckled at the thought of what he was about to do. Shaking his head, Dade picked up his feet, and went for what he knew before he could rationalize. Otherwise, he'd reconsider, and sit his ass back down. The entrance to the women's room became closer with each step taken. Just as his feet crossed the threshold of the private space, designated for women only, SaeKu came crashing into Dade.

His chest swelled, repelling against her major hit. Dropping her luggage handle, it fell to the floor as she held her hands in the air. "Sorry." She still hadn't realized just who she'd bumped into. Head near the ground, she searched for her things that had fallen.

Leaning forward, Dade grabbed the handle to her luggage and picked it up from the ground. "It's all good, SaeKu. I wanted to talk to you..."

Words cut short, remarks caught in his throat, and thoughts jumbled, Dade's heart filled with grief as SaeKu looked up at the sound of his voice. Feeling as little demons were piercing his chest with splinters, physical pain consumed him even more than emotional. SaeKu's previously white rims were red in color, and her perfect skin was now blemished. A damsel in distress, her nostrils were inflated, signaling an onset of emotions.

She.... She couldn't have...

Dade took a second for things to resonate.

Without second thought, Dade grabbed SaeKu by the arm. Looking over his shoulder, he pushed her towards the men's restroom with her luggage in tow. Before she could protest, SaeKu's back was against the wall and her Dade's hands were around her neck –in a very sensual way. With his face buried in between her neck and shoulder, he inhaled the scent that he'd reminisced about on many nights.

She smelled just as he recalled. He'd missed her so much, and wanted her to understand that nothing had changed between the two. Circumstances, maybe, but his feelings remained the same. After seeing her face, he was reminded of the fact. Unlike any other time, he wouldn't let up until they both explored everything that there was to between one another.

The tears in her beautiful brown eyes exposed an untold story, one that Dade had never heard. Yet, he wanted to know what it was all about. Sure that it was magnificent in every sense of the word, he only prayed that he was allowed the pleasure of it's melodies. Turning the very first page, unintentionally, Dade gaged a reaction that he wasn't half expecting from SaeKu.

"FUCK." Dade called out, barely above a whisper.

"You said you'd wait." SaeKu finally broke her silence. Damping Dade's black sweat shirt with the moisture that pooled at his shoulders.

Damn...

He thought to himself.

"I did. I waited. I waited, aight. I'm still waiting. I ran... I chased you... Look at us, now. I'm still chasing you. Say the word and this shit is history." Dade lifted his head, and stepped backwards, being sure that SaeKu understood the seriousness of his statement.

SaeKu's eyes darted across the restroom, realizing they weren't alone. In fact, they were accompanied by at least ten other men, who seemed to be paying them no mind. As they handled their business, pissing all over the urinals, no one paid them any attention.

"Don't you dare." SaeKu chastised Dade with a finger. Her natural pink coffin shaped nails were inches from his caramel colored skin. Wanting to reach out and caress the side of his face, SaeKu reminded herself to stand her ground. "I would never ask you to leave your family."

"SaeKu, you've got it all wrong." Dade threw his hands in the arm.

"No, Dade." SaeKu yanked away, upset that Dade had even placed himself in such a permanent predicament. How would they ever get passed that. It was impossible, and SaeKu wanted no parts in it.

This shit was ugly, and it pained just to know that someone else would be bearing his child. It pained even worse to know that he'd given up on her, and given someone else what he'd once promised her. A child was the ultimate, and SaeKu could barely believe it, less known accept it.

"You've got me all wrong." She straightened her attire, and grabbed her luggage.

"Na." Dade forcefully pulled her back, and slammed her against the wall.

Her back hit the concrete with a thud, but before she could respond, her lips were covered with his. Closing her eyes, SaeKu fell into the moment, surrendering to the power that Dade reigned over her. Wanting so badly for him to be her reality, she knew that he'd never be more than a beautiful dream that she had, and that was the only space that they'd rightfully share together. Pulling back, SaeKu wiped her lips, embarrassed by her submissiveness.

"I have a plane to catch." SaeKu tugged at her luggage.

This time, Dade allowed her to turn and leave. Dialing into the cell in his hand, he waited for a ring. Just as SaeKu made it to the exit of the restroom, the cell in her pocket rang. Reaching inside of it, she pulled it out, realizing the pink case that she had protecting it was replaced with a gray one. Turning back, she rolled her eyes into the back of her head and sighed. Dade had switched cells with her. He refused to leave empty handed, not knowing if it would be another year before they crossed paths again. Smirking, he stretched his hand out to give her the phone that she owned, still covered in pink.

"Answer when I call. I want to clear this all up, but this isn't the time or place. Don't shut me out this time. I don't deserve it. Quite frankly, I never have. Fuck with me if you want to, and I will clear each crevice of the United States until I find your ass." Tapping her chest with

his index fingers, Dade continued. "You've got a few matters at heart, but we're going to work through them together."

Snatching her phone, she replaced it with Dade's phone, and made her way out into the busy airport. As she walked, head hung, she allowed her tears to fall onto the shoes of anyone in her path. Heartbroken and confused, SaeKu felt something that she never had, ***replaceable****. It was the single worst feeling that a woman could possess when it pertained to a man that she actually craved in every sense of the word.*

Although time had gotten in the way, there wasn't a day that his brown skin didn't cross her visual. Now, not only was her heart crushed, but her womanhood had been revoked – prematurely. What had started out as a pretty decent day had quickly become one of the worst of her living. Slumping her shoulders, SaeKu slithered to her next assignment, Dade sitting at the head of her mental.

"That's what I'm talking about, son!" Lorde cheered his cousin on.

"Man, I still feel like shit." Dade released a long breath and placed his hands on his knees. Looking behind him, he made sure that Alani was still in the shower. Hearing the water running confirmed things for him.

"You should, nigga. I would've been screaming… That baby ain't mine." Lorde joked.

"Shut the hell up." Lorde shook his head. "You're no help at all, here."

"Motherfuckers never want to hear the truth." Lorde shrugged. He was so blunt that it was nearly ridiculous at times.

"It wasn't the time, Lorde. Besides, I told you about that one time."

"Fuck that one time. You're too formal and shit. I would've been straight up… Not to mention, I would've gave her some act right in that bathroom. You had the perfect timing and all. Had that little attendant uniform hiked up, making that shit squeak." Lorde dry humped his leather seats, mimicking how he would've been had he been Dade.

"I don't even know why I called your ass. Nigga you are missing some screws." Dade chuckled, finally letting up on himself a little.

"That's okay though. As long as you're equip with all of yours, then I'm good."

"How is mama?" Lorde changed the subject.

"Tripping out. Call her. She was on one, tonight."

"When is she never on one?"

"She knows that Alani is with me?"

"Yeah."

"Fuck that. I'll holler at her when I get back." Dade waved the thought off. There was no way in hell he was calling his mother with knowing that she was well aware of who'd accompanied him on his vacation.

Lorde burst into laughter. Dade wasn't confrontational at all, especially when it came to their mother. "Shakey ass nigga."

"Whatever man. I'll hit you back when I touch down."

"One."

"One."

"You okay?" Alani asked Dade. She'd been calling his name for over twenty seconds, and he had just responded.

"Um… Yeah." He nodded. "You ready?" he questioned.

"Yeah. I don't look too fat do I?"

"You're pregnant. Are you trying to look skinny or some shit?" Dade shrugged, all of a sudden agitated with her presence. "My bad." He paused as he realized how harsh that sounded. "I've got a lot of shit on my mind."

"Obviously." Alani was completely thrown off by his response.

Walking off, she opened the door to their beautiful cottage, which was located at the water's edge. They were meeting the clan for a late dinner, being that everyone was too tired a few hours earlier to do anything but get settled and rest.

"Alani," Dade caught up to her, treading along the sand.

"Yeah, Dade?" She turned to face him.

Knowing that none of this her fault, he softened. The moment he looked into her deep brown eyes, he wanted to warn her of the reappearance of SaeKu. However, he didn't want to spoil her trip. The baby was due in three months, and this would be her last vacation. Dade didn't want to be the one to ruin it.

"My bad. You look beautiful." He retracted his statement from earlier.

He wasn't lying either. Her honey colored skin glistened under the settling sun. The body moisturizer that she'd covered herself in had a light shimmer, and glitter like particles reflected – giving her skin a glowing effect.

"Thanks," she blushed, her one dimple causing Dade to smile.

Alani and SaeKu were polar opposites. Whereas SaeKu was combative by nature, Alani was cooperative in every way. SaeKu was dark like the dead of the night, and Alani resembled the rays of the sun on a bright sunny day. Light brown tresses hung just at her shoulders, but she kept them tucked under custom made wigs and protective styles. A diva in every way, Alani was rarely caught looking anything less than decent. Even at the grocery store, she was well groomed, and ready for the runway.

"How are you feeling?"

"I'm good. We're good." Alani rubbed her stomach. "What about you?"

"I'm good, baby." Dade kissed her forehead, and squeezed both of her arms.

Closing his eyes, SaeKu's tear stained skin flashed before them. Quickly opening them back, he pulled away from Alani. Grabbing her hand, he walked her towards the tent that was reserved for their dinner. Closing his eyes once more, Dade hoped that a more pleasing image of SaeKu would replace the previous one, but there was no suck luck. Again, she showed with the same worried eyes as he'd left her with.

"DADE!" Keem noticed the couple the minute they entered.

Spilling her drink from her lips, Reed choked on the little that had seeped down the wrong pipe. Bella's eyes bulged from her sockets, and her hand immediately went into her purse. It was as if it was a natural reflex.

KinZu, on the other hand, had no reaction to the realization that Dade had obviously moved on, and stopped waiting around for her sister. She'd told her to cut her bullshit long ago. Now, she was much too late. He was with child, and had a beautiful young woman to share the experience with.

"What's good, yo?"

"I can't call it. Glad you could join us. We're making this an annual thing, so get used to this shit."

"Don't worry. That's the aim. I want to introduce everyone to my… to Alani." Dade quickly recouped, choosing a different set of words. In no way did he want to introduce Alani as his woman, even with it being the truth. Declaring it amongst a room full of SaeKu's family was unheard of.

"Nice to meet you, Alani. How far along?"

"Month seven." Alani smiled. "And you are?"

"KinZu. You can call me Kin. You want to come over here with us women? The men are somewhere plotting, and Keem can't seem to stop sniffing up his wife's ass for two seconds to let her breathe." KinZu threw over her shoulder as she pulled Alani along –never waiting for her response.

Looking back at Dade, she waited for his approval. Nodding, he let her know that she'd be alright.

"Baby, we don't want you. We're strictly dickly over here. You don't have to ask Dade ass for approval." Bella said, harshly, taking a sip of her long island ice tea –which had her feeling a bit brutal. Not bothering to look up from her phone, she continued to read SaeKu in what seemed like a four-page letter –via text.

"Excuse her. She's drunk. I'm Reed, and that's my husband, Keem." Reed extended her hand, and walked closer to Alani. The two shook as Dade eased out of the tent. Reed didn't miss the snickering from her husband, on Alani's expense.

"Nice to meet you." Alani took the hint, and ignored Bella's rudeness. She was a girl with tough skin, so she let her remarks roll off of her shoulders.

"Same here. Wine, maybe?"

"As long as it's red. I'll take a glass. Just one." Alani was sure to include.

Bella stared at Alani under her lids, trying to read her. Unfortunately, she was met with not a bit of resistance. Her spirits told her that Alani was nothing like she had prejudged. Not wanting to give in to the initial reading, Bella vowed to keep a close eye on her.

"So, how was your flight?"

"It was cool. Dade slept nearly the entire time. He'd been up half of the night trying to figure out which companies he would chose to invest in. Before we knew it, it was time to head out of the house. Well, we went by his mother's grave before departure."

"His mother's grave?" Reed was shocked at the revelation that Dade's mother was deceased. He'd mentioned his mother on more than one occasion, so this left her a bit baffled.

"Yeah."

"That's wild. He's never mentioned the death of his mother. I'm going to have to make sure that I offer my condolences." Reed was left with a bitter taste in her mouth. According to her thoughts, they were a bit closer to Dade than anyone. She felt as if they would've know about the death of his mother.

"Yeah, my baby is a bit sensitive about the subject." Alani pursed her lips, and watched as Dade threw his head back in laughter, joking amongst his boys.

The sound of her calling Dade anything other than his name caused Bella to nearly hurl. Standing from her comfortable position, she allowed her sheer cover up to swing open, exposing her beautifully tanned skin. Body sickening after two children, still, Bella was sure to set the tone high for post baby standards.

"I have an important call to make." Bella announced.

"Yeah, I think that I'd better check on Rance." Reed agreed to make a call as well.

"I guess that's my cue, too. My two are probably missing me something awful." Wise thought of her babies, and cooed. Although they were both up in age, she still considered them to be her babies –and they would forever be.

"Now you guys are making me feel bad for not wanting to call my three piece." Kelly whined. "I don't even feel like hearing their voices."

"Oh, don't worry. We all know your pain. Just come on get it out of the way, and then we won't have to call these little critters for the rest of our vacation." Bella shrugged.

"You're right about that one." Kelly nodded.

The women filed in the house, without either of their children on their mental. In fact, the grandparents had all taken the children on a vacation to Disney. They'd met, and was staying in the family resort. Meek's mother, Bella's mother, and Liam's grandmother were all kicked back with the children and insisted that their mother's left them the hell alone.

"Call that little bitch right now!" Wise walked into the house, slamming her designer shades on the counter.

"What the hell is she thinking?" Reed questioned, snatching over the fridge in search of more food.

"Reed, I keep telling you to check with your doctor. Either you have a worm that's eating a hole in your ass, or that's another Keem on the way." Bella waved her hand in the air, dismissing Reed's comment before she could even get her thoughts together.

Her cell chimed as she leaned on the counter. "I'm not even texting her back. I'm calling." Bella didn't even do as much as glance at the message that SaeKu had sent. She was in no mood for her shenanigans.

"SaeKu Noble." Bella belted into the phone.

"Put her ass on speaker. I want to hear this shit." Kelly folded her arms and leaned backwards. Closing her eyes, she tried to tune everyone out, but SaeKu.

"Yes, Bella."

"I hope that you have some mileage and some bikinis, because you're coming to this island like yesterday."

"No I'm not."

"Dade is here!" Kelly yelled across the room.

Covering her phone, Bella hoped that SaeKu hadn't heard what was being said. If she knew that Dade was around, there was no way she was coming. Silence sliced the connection that Bella had made with SaeKu, and the phone went dead. "Did she hang up on me?" Bella questioned.

"I think so."

Dialing her back, Bella fanned her forehead, and mugged her screen as she waited for it to alert her that SaeKu was back on the line. Bella was quick on her feet. The minute that SaeKu picked up, she was on her ass. "I mean, the flight wasn't so bad. I don't mind getting a round trip back to the states, and bringing you back with me."

"Bella. Please. I told you the first time that I'm not coming. It's a couple's retreat. I don't have a man remember!"

"You would if you'd stop the fooling around and get up with what's his name." Bella chuckled, waving her hand at the girls to get their attention.

“Well, it’s a little too late for that.” SaeKu’s voice pained.

“What do you mean?” Bella became concerned, sensing the uneasy tone in SaeKu’s voice.

“I saw him, today.” SaeKu sighed. “And he wasn’t alone. I really fucked this one up, Bella.”

“Don’t say that. Where did you see him?” Bella stood straight and leaned against the wall.

“He was in-flight. I nearly lost my marbles.”

“I’m sure you did. How are you feeling? What happened? Tell me more, hell.”

“There’s nothing to tell, honestly. He wanted to talk it out, but I won’t be answering when he calls. He’s already on the blocked list.”

“Don’t give up so easily. Maybe this is just a thing for him. He waited for you. The least you can do is hear him out.”

“Bella, I can’t compete with a child. I wouldn’t even want to set myself up like that.”

“You’re right about that. But hey! Look at it like this… That gives you all the more reasons to come and chill. It’s beautiful out here, SaeKu. Don’t make me come get you.”

“Will you just knock it off?”

“NO!” Bella yelled in the phone. Wise was pumping her up in the background. Now, they were all on board with getting her to come on. The rekindling would be beautiful to say the least.

“Bella.”

“Don’t Bella me. You got that damn flight attendant job eight months ago, and you’ve been up in the air ever since. Take a day or two off and kick it with your family. We haven’t seen you since yester-years." Bella was not letting up. Her spirits were leading, and she was following.

"Whatever Bella." SaeKu sighed.

"So, you're coming?"

"Yeah. I have one more assignment, and then I'll be on the way."

"Is Sage coming?"

"Sage may come tomorrow. She'll be working through the night."

"Good. Good. I'm excited. Only bring your best shit. If you need me to, then I'll shop before you get here."

"That sounds like a better idea. Otherwise, I'll be heading back to New York to pack a bag."

"We can't have that. The girls and I will have you right. Don't worry. Oh yeah, this vacation is on me. I'm reimbursing you."

"You don't have to do that!" SaeKu yelled into the receiver.

"I insist." Bella ended the calls and the girls all slapped hands.

"Dade is going to kill us."

"No he isn't. He'll probably be happy. Seems like he wanted to iron out the kinks when he saw her earlier." Wise winked.

"I can't believe he's actually here. I'm surprised he didn't cancel after seeing her. That girl has a hold on him like no other." Reed added.

"But he is… And he's here with some hoochie with a big belly."

"Really Bella?" Wise questioned, folding her arms. "Now, nothing about that girl says hoochie. The girl is expecting for crying out loud. What has she done to you?"

"She came here with Dade. Shit that's enough. She should know better. I'm tired of these women committing to the side chick role. It's tasteless and tacky on their behalf. That's no way to live." Bella threw her hands in the air and blew out a frustrated breath.

"Bella. How is she the side chick, though?" Reed questioned, throwing a few chips into her mouth.

"I don't know. Go ask her." Bella couldn't help but to laugh at her own antics.

"Bella." Kelly chuckled.

"No. Don't Bella me. Grab your men American Express cards. We're going shopping."

"But what about dinner?" Reed was dumbfounded.

"What about dinner?" Bella shrugged. "You can go play nice, but I'm in no mood. I have to make sure that our girl is on point when she makes it here."

"Well bye. I'm staying, and I'm eating. I can care less about who's on the side of me."

"With your pregnant ass." Kelly yelled back. "Aight, before you know it you'll be on baby number five."

"Kelly. Bella. I'm not pregnant. Let me breathe, damn." Reed rushed out of the house. Her bare feet connected with the sand, sinking as she took each step. "Keem." She yelled out to her husband, near tears.

The distress in his wife's voice alarmed him. The young couple had a two-and-a-half-year old daughter, had been married for three years, and Reed was on the verge of losing it with thoughts running rapid of a baby number two. She'd been avoiding the topic for weeks, but with Bella and Kelly monitoring her moves, she could no longer hide the frustration.

Jumping from his seat, Keem met Reed halfway, knowing that she was less than thrilled. "What's up, baby?" he questioned.

"Come here."

Reed pulled her husband's shirt until they were on the side of their cabana. Before she could speak, tears swelled in her eyes. Focusing on her pedicured toes, she bowed her head and swiped her face free of residue.

"Talk to me." Keem rubbed Reed's back. "What's gotten you upset?"

"Maybe…" Reed started. Looking up into her husband's eyes, she continued. "Maybe, I'm pregnant. I don't really know, but I…"

"Seriously?" Keem beamed. His voice was a bit louder than Reed would've liked. The thrill in his tone irked her, but she didn't have the guts to admit the fact. "We're going to have another baby?"

"Keem. Calm down. I didn't say that. I said, "Maybe." Besides, don't get too worked up. You know what happened the first time." Reed reminded him of the child that they'd miscarried.

"I'm not going to let you ruin my spirits with that, and you're not going to let that get you down either. We had Rance, and she is fine."

"But still. These pregnancies are pretty risky, Keem."

"And just like we got through one, we can get through another. Lighten up. Is this what the tears are about?" Keem stood off to the side to have a good look at his wife. "Or am I missing something?"

"No." Reed lied. She didn't bother looking Keem in his eyes, because she knew he'd call her out on her shit. Little did she know, that was his intentions, anyway.

"I think I am. Are you out here weeping like a little bitch because you think you're pregnant with your husband's child, or is it really the fact that you're concerned with your health –in the event that you are carrying my seed?" Keem moved closer to Reed, daring her to say the wrong thing.

"Keem." She chastised him for his choice of words.

"Keem shit, Reed." Keem raised a brow. "Now, tell me what the issue is here, because I see nothing worth crying about."

Without a response, Keem understood the nature of her displeasing mode. It wasn't her health or the health of an unborn that she was concerned with. It was the news in itself. Keem would be lying if he'd ever said daggers didn't pierce his heart as he watched his beautiful wife fold under his intense glare.

"Yo!" Keem stared, but couldn't find the right words.

Instead of speaking, he opted to wave his hand dismissively. Reed reached out, and tried grabbing his shirt, wanting him to understand her reservations. He showed no interest as he shooed her claws from his cloth, and went to join his tribe –once again.

Peeking around the cabana, Reed could tell by the way that Keem's shoulders sunk that her thoughts were weighing heavy on his heart. Sighing, Reed looked down at her abdomen section, and then back to her husband.

"Well. It's not like there's anything I can do about it." She shrugged, and made her way back into the space that her girls were now dispensing from.

Chapter Two

The sun rose before SaeKu arrived on the secluded island full of friend's and family. As she walked into the main house, her stomach growled at the smell of food. Sleep had been the furthest from her mind upon seeing the girls in the kitchen going to town. Guessing the men had all slept in, SaeKu joined Bella, Wise, Kelly, KinZu, and Reed in the kitchen. Immediately washing her hands, she asked where she could lend a hand.

"Good morning. Where can I start?" SaeKu beamed. She was genuinely happy to be amongst family and friends.

"Well isn't this a pleasant surprise." KinZu turned from the sink, rinsing bacon, when she heard her sister's voice.

Rolling her eyes to the top of her head, Bella ignored KinZu's sarcasm, and answered SaeKu's question. "Here. Throw this over you. We're happy that you decided to join us. We figured you'd be in bed the better part of the day." Bella chunked SaeKu an apron, much like the ones that decorated each woman's chest that stood in the kitchen.

Looking around, SaeKu observed the tanned beauties and smiled. Conclusively, she figured they'd been bathing under the rays of the gorgeous island sun the previous evening.

Fortunately, it had them all resembling exotics. Focusing on her very own skin, she wondered if it was even possible to darken more.

"If you'd like, you can cut the veggies for the omelets." Wise insisted. "That's about all that is left to do."

"Sounds like a plan to me." SaeKu clapped her hands together, and went in search of a suitable knife.

"So, SaeKu, when did you get in?" KinZu questioned.

"Not even two hours ago. I went to tuck my things away, and then came back to the main hub." SaeKu shrugged. "I'm actually glad I came. It's so beautiful here."

And it was. The Jamaican island was traced with rich sand that engulfed your toes, and covered your feet upon contact. The big green trees stood over 12 feet tall, with coconuts and exotic fruit hanging from many. The water that traced the border of their exclusive getaway looked crystal clear, with a hint of sky blue peeking through the waves.

Their secluded area allowed them to see into the city, and it was amazing seeing how locals carried about their day. From their private space, the couples could see the festivities of the city during the night.

"It is. It's very refreshing." Kelly nodded.

Reed was without concern for the conversations of activities being administered amongst everyone in the kitchen. Her mind was consumed with thoughts of Keem, who'd slept in the living area of their cabana. Reed had tried, for the better part of the night, to force him to bed, but he wouldn't budge.

"Especially with the view of the city. To see how other cultures live is just awesome. Liam and I watched them party from our gazebo." Wise smiled.

"Roc and I watched from the window. They can really get down." Kelly chuckled.

"Right. We're going to have to go join them one night before we go back." Bella assured them. "Rub this ass on some Jamaican dick."

"And have a nigga catching a case. Don't get these Jamaican niggas killed." Meek appeared from thin air, and kissed his wife's cheek. His eyes landed on SaeKu, and confusion covered his forehead. "What's up? When did you get here?" Meek asked.

Pulling open the fridge, he grabbed the carton of orange juice, and was handed a cup. Bella knew her husband like the back of her hand.

"This morning." SaeKu answered. "Hand me a cup, too, Bella. I could use something to quench this thirst. My throat is screaming." SaeKu joked.

"Are you gracing our entire stay with your presence?" Meek joked, but honestly wanted to know her plans.

With Dade complaining about the nature of their relationship throughout the entire night, he was wondering if they were aware of each other's presence. He also wanted to be nosey, and see how the fuck Dade would handle both of his women being on the island together.

Although he and SaeKu had never made anything official, everyone knew what was up. There wasn't any denying the bond that had been created between the two. Even though they'd never been exclusive, their importance in one another's life went without saying.

"I'm thinking three days. You guys will be here for five more. I can't take that much time. I had someone to cover me one of those days. I can't afford to miss anymore."

"Understood. Get that dough." Meek nodded, raising his cup, kissing his wife's forehead, and heading back out.

Placing the cup to her lips, SaeKu recalled the exhilaration that soared through her veins as Dade blessed her with forehead kisses. His succulent lips guided her to heaven, momentarily. A soft moan fell from SaeKu's lips as she slipped down memory lane. Muffling her sounds, she gulped the orange juice that sat at her lips.

"Good morning." Alani pounced into the kitchen with a burst of energy that could brighten the darkest room. She'd rested well, and was ready to take on the day. Her lightly colored tresses hung past her shoulders, as she sauntered –causing the flowing sundress to sway with each movement.

The thick orange liquid flew from SaeKu's mouth as the strings on her heart tugged, causing physical damage. With sweaty palms, SaeKu placed the glass on the counter, and attempted to get control of her coughing. With one hand planted on the counter, and the other around her neck, she tried to regulate her breathing. Surprisingly, she'd stopped remembering to do so at some point.

Seeing Alani was not expected, and SaeKu was thrown completely left. Her presence could only mean one thing. Dade was on the island as well. SaeKu's insides flamed at the revelation that she'd be moping around for the next three days, rather than vacationing as she'd planned.

"Oh God, are you okay?" Alani asked, rushing to SaeKu's rescue.

Alani happened to be the closest, being that she was on her way to the fridge. Patting SaeKu's back, she assisted her in her time of despair. As she rubbed SaeKu back to good health, she looked up to see Dade walking into the kitchen.

SaeKu lifted, face strained, and eyes bulging from her socket. She placed her hand on her chest, and took slow and deep breaths. "It's you!" Alani spoke. "The flight attendant."

"Blogger and future choreographer." Bella added. "We can't forget to add that."

Wise bit into the cream cheesed bagel she'd prepared, refusing to burst into a fit of laugher like she wanted.

"Right. Can't forget that." Kelly clapped.

Clearing his throat, Dade turned to make his exit before SaeKu could set her sights on him. His bluff was called when Alani yelled out to him, informing him that their flight attendant had made it all the way to Jamaica.

"Baby. Look who's here. It's such a coincident."

Yeah. About that. Bitch, she was coming before you were. Bella interfered, in her head, at least.

"Yeah. Alani. What's up, SaeKu?" Dade greeted with a nod of the head.

"I had no clue that you two knew one another. Small world."

"Too fucking small if you ask me." Kelly threw her hands in the air, slightly agitated with Dade's nonchalant attitude. "Let me go round up the rest of the guys and let them know that we'll be ready in ten."

"Yeah. Don't worry about the vegetables, SaeKu. I can use the ones left over from the hash browns."

Dade's grits seemed to grow thicker each time he shoved his spoon into the mix. While the entire family chatted and brought back old memories, his feelings had plummeted. For the second time in less than 48 hours, he'd thrown his made-up relationship in the face of the woman that he truly loved.

Cutting his eyes to the left of him, he gazed at the pained expression that SaeKu wore on her face. Her laughter was forced and her smile was nonexistent. She was dying inside, and he wasn't man enough to breathe into her the air that she needed to live. He'd, selfishly, snatched away her supply, and given it to someone who didn't rightfully deserve it.

Feeling a pair of eyes hovering over her, she turned. Both Dade and SaeKu became lost in one another. All that wanted to be said was, and all that needed to be forgiven was. The temporarily elapse of judgment and truths connected their souls and joined them as time should have.

"I left my meds back at our place." Alani barked, breaking the intensity of Dade's stare. "Baby, I need to go and get them. I'll be back in a bit. I'm going to freshen up while I'm there. I think that I am done, here." Alani stood from her seat at the table.

Bending over, she kissed Dade on his lips, and then his forehead. His response was delayed, and nearly nonexistent. While sending Alani on her way, his eyes found SaeKu, again. A sarcastic grin was plastered on her lips as she stared into the sky.

"SaeKu, let me holler at you." Dade's voice boomed the minute Alani made her exit.

"Na, player." SaeKu chuckled. "Bella, I thank you guys for the breakfast, but I think that I am done, here. Let me know when everyone is getting out. I'll be in attendance."

SaeKu dismissed herself from the table after grabbing her plate, which was partially full. She'd lost her appetite before grace was recited, and heads were bowed. The growing pain in the pit of her stomach nearly forced every piece of food that she'd managed to get down right back up.

Dade's eye roamed the table, questionably. Every man in attendance nodded their heads towards SaeKu, confirming exactly what Dade knew was required of him, the implementation of authority. It was necessary that he put his foot down, or SaeKu would continue to have him by the balls.

Throwing his spoon onto his plate, Dade jumped up from his seat, hot on SaeKu's trail. She could hear his steps behind her, breaking every barrier that she'd placed in front of him. His cologne lingered in the air, making her juice box water and her resolve less hard. SaeKu threw her dish into the sink, and turned to make her exit. However, she was met with resistance.

Dade's handsome face was complex, and filled with grief as he flexed his jaws. Grabbing her by the arm, Dade directed her out of the kitchen and onto the back deck.

Snatching away, SaeKu started to walk off. She couldn't stand the look on his face or the tone in his voice when he called out her name, "SAEKU!" he said through gritted teeth. Pulling her backwards, she fell into his chest.

"I'm sorry." He admitted, grabbing the back of her head, and forcing her to look up at him. "You have to believe that shit."

He was killing her softly with his words, the look on his face, the grip on her hair, the smell of his cologne, and overflow of love that exuded from his frame. "Do you hear me?" he questioned, grabbing her lips and squeezing them apart. Stuffing his tongue down her throat, he didn't give her much room to defy him.

Breathing shallow and heart pounding, SaeKu pulled backwards. "I love you!"

The words emerged from her lips like a baby from it's mother's wombs. She birth a new sector of emotions and embarked on a new journey with the simple, yet meaningful, phrase that was usually preached under different circumstances. "Didn't you ever see that?" Tears cascaded down her beautiful brown cheeks. "You said that you would wait!"

"I did. I'm still waiting. I'm still chasing. Look at us, now!" Dade pointed between the two. His words were backed by passion. He'd just heard the most rejuvenating words that he'd ever been blessed with. His ears were still ringing from the announcement –heart throbbing and chest burning. Guessing this is what love felt like, Dade wondered why the hell he hadn't fell for it sooner.

"No. You didn't wait. You settled. You went with what was easier. This only proves my point. I'm just too fucking complicated." SaeKu waved her hands as if she'd pushed them into a burning furnace and brought them back out. "Let's just be real here, Dade. Maybe we were meant to be in one another's life, but not in the way that we both want."

"SaeKu, you don't know what the fuck you want." Dade countered.

"How dare you?" SaeKu's chest swelled. "My soul needed fixing, and getting cozy with you wouldn't have made it any better. Depression is real, Dade. It's not some concoction of the white man. I was drowning, and no one around me seemed to notice."

"I was trying to save you." Dade pleaded.

"I didn't need saving." SaeKu yelled. "I needed healing. I needed to find a way to heal before I through my burdens on your back. I needed to learn to stand on my own for once. I needed patience, love, and care. I needed you. Even if not at the moment, I still needed you. I needed you to be there when I got my shit together."

"I'm right here."

"Don't you dare insult me." SaeKu raised a finger. "You're not here. You're there."

"SaeKu, what the fuck do you expect from a nigga? I got a whole dick that needs to be fucked and sucked on a daily. Waiting on you, and a nigga would've been old and gray before you came back around. To be real, I think that only reason you expressing what you feel is because someone is willing to be everything that you wanted to be for me, but didn't have the fucking balls to commit to." Dade called her bluff. Folding his arms, he waited for a response.

Turning on her heels, SaeKu recanted the statement that she'd made earlier –replacing it with fiery. "I fucking hate you!" she yelled. Storming off, she headed back towards the house.

Again, Dade was hot on her trail, slamming her against the brick wall, next to the back door. "Take that shit back." He warned, grabbing her chin.

"Get the fuck off of me!" SaeKu cried. "Just go!" her heart broke into little shards of glass, cutting Dade at the center of his most valuable vessel.

"I can't." he admitted. "Not until you take that shit back." His shoulders slummed. "I can't have you out here giving a nigga life and then snatching it back like that."

His New York accent was heavy enough to weigh down SaeKu's eyelids. As she closed them, she felt hands entangle with her arms. Her neck and shoulder were both introduced to heat, from slow breathing on Dade's end. "Take that shit back." He repeated, lowering his hand to SaeKu's source of sweet salvation.

"Stop." SaeKu's fingers dug into Dade's back, as he rubbed her pussy through the cloth that blocked his fingers from feeling her soft flesh.

"Take it back." He repeated.

"Sto…" SaeKu's mouth fell open as she felt Dade's other hand being removed from her body. Seconds later, she heard his linen bottoms unzip. Her panties filled with sweet nectar at the thought of being stroked by the glorious member that awaited her.

Seconds felt like a lifetime, but that was merely the case. Dade was in just as much of a rush to be back inside of his home as SaeKu was. As his heated tip thumped at her opening, SaeKu grasped. She'd been hoisted into the air, and her hands were wrapped around Dade's neck when he dove into her treasure. A satisfied sigh left their lips, simultaneously.

"Take it back." Dade remained still, unable to move.

Had he fulfilled her wishes, their journey would've ended before it started. The same way that she felt the very first time he entered her hidden oasis, she still felt. It was as if she had a magic potion coated pussy that was destined to bring him to his knees, crying like a little bitch.

He'd wanted nothing more than to scream out to his maker upon entrance. Afterwards, a back rub and thumb to the mouth would soothe him –putting him right to sleep. Dade was certain that he'd feel like a new born, gone off of the breast milk once his wand was emptied, and SaeKu had drained the life out of him with barely any effort.

SaeKu's head fell backwards, and her body began to float on thin air. Up and down, she rode Dade's shaft. His moans were in resemblance of low whines. His please went unanswered as SaeKu continued to hold onto his neck, using the brick wall for support. Her exotic features were too much to bare, with her exotic pussy taking him beyond oblivion. Closing his eyes, Dade held on to the wall to keep from giving in with his knees, making them both fall onto the ground.

"Stop being so fucking nosey!" Meek snuck up on Bella, and scared the shit out of her.

Dropping her plate into the sink, she turned and punched him in the chest. "Don't scare me like that Meek. Besides, I had a great view of the show."

He chuckled, and pulled her into his arms. As she buried her head into his chest, he stole a peep out into the backyard. It took his eyes a few seconds to adjust to the sight before him. Dade's eyes were shut tight as SaeKu gave his ass the blues. Smiling, Meek nodded his head, and backed up into the eating area.

"You see that shit?" Bella whispered.

"Hell yeah. Them motherfuckers wild."

As Bella turned to motion for Kelly's attention, Alani appeared. Her smile dropped once realizing Dade had disappeared. Looking up to KinZu, her only pal since she'd been there, she asked, "Hey. Where did the Mr. go?"

"He's handling some unfinished business." Kelly chimed in before KinZu could conjure up an answer.

"Unfinished business?" Alani giggled, nervously, noticing the fact that SaeKu, too, had come up missing.

"Yeah. That nigga will be back in a minute." Meek cleared her assumptions with a quick input.

Bella, Reed, Kelly, and Wise all gave each other approving nods. Their plan wasn't full proof, but it was proving to work to some degree. While Alani was questioning her beloved Dade's whereabouts, he was less than 200 feet away, making love to his dear SaeKu.

On the back deck of the house, Dade buried himself into SaeKu's warmth over and over, again. As he reached his peak, he gripped her tresses, and forced her to recant her statement. "Take that shit back." He repeated for the umpteenth time.

"I love you." SaeKu grunted as she poured her flavored liquid onto his extra thick growing. "I love you."

The words shot daggers through Dade's chest, resting right at his heart. It was true, she loved him. There wasn't a doubt in his mind that combatted her confession. With hesitation on his brain and a wholesome feeling radiating through his heart, Dade responded in the only way that he felt necessary.

"… I love the fuck out of you, too, girl." He removed himself from her opening, and allowed his seeds to gather on the wooden planks below their feet. "Shit." He called out at the sight of Alani.

**

"Where did you go?" Alani asked when Dade walked into their temporary dwelling.

"I had some shit to handle." Dade was suddenly confronted with the agitation of her presence once more. She hadn't done anything, but the fact that it was her not doing anything rather than SaeKu was the root of his irritancy.

"Is everything okay?" She questioned, sensing his attitude.

"It will be. What's up with the questions?"

"Just trying to make sure you're good." Alani shrugged.

"I'm good." Dade assured her. "I need to hop in the shower before we get a start on our day."

"We took a shower before breakfast."

"And when I went to handle shit, it required a clean up afterwards. Now, do you mind me taking a shower, or you want me to walk around without cleaning myself up?" Dade wore a smudge look on his face.

"Go ahead, Dade."

Alani continued to look through her suitcase, trying to find the bottom to her swimsuit. Her attempts failed miserably as her tears filled her pretty brown rounds. Her mind was traveling a mile a minute. Her insides burned as she came to grips with the obvious. What was supposed to be a pleasurable trip has turned disastrous, almost immediately.

Alani was a woman, and their intuitions were hardly ever wrong. Vomit neared the top of her throat as she thought back onto how love struck Dade was the minute he laid eyes on the flight attendant. Not to mention, while in-flight, he'd disappeared for nearly 20 minutes. Coincidentally, the same attendant had been whisked to an entirely different country, and it happened to be the same one they were visiting. Not to mention the disappearance of the two, simultaneously.

The evil glares and backlash that she was receiving from the women in company was all beginning to make sense. Dade needing a shower was like icing on a caramel covered ice cream cake. He'd confirmed every suspicion that she'd swatted away minutes prior. As fucked up as it was, she had no plans of leaving the island, or Dade for the matter. Wiping her tears with the back of her hand, Alani coached herself into a peaceful mood. The mere thought of not being in Dade's presence hurt worse than any other feeling Alani had ever come in contact with.

**

The night fell as SaeKu entered her private dwelling. Bella had reserved the space after she'd agreed to accompany the clan. Tossing her bag onto the floor, she fell over onto the bed. The six-hour flight, plus the miles she'd flown to cover her shift, island activities, and dodging the likes of Dade had drained her. Sighing, she pondered whether to shower, or get comfortable in bed.

Thirty minutes later, and she was emerging from the shower, towel drying her loosely curled tresses. The moonlight shined through the bay window, causing her to stare momentarily.

If only my life could be as simple and amazing as the moonlight. SaeKu pursed her lips, and threw the damp towel onto the floor. Seating herself on the bed, she logged into her playlist and begin to let the sounds of, "Lose My Mind," by Janine and The Mixtape rock her world.

As she dressed for the night, Dade invaded her thoughts. All day, his newest companionship had been thrust in her face. At a time or two, she'd felt the urge to puke. So loving and gentle, Dade was the ultimate prize. SaeKu was overcome with grief, as she mourned the possibility of never being able experience the love that Dade had once offered her.

Tossing him out of her mind, she prepared the sheets for laying. Tomorrow was a new day, and Sage would be pulling in. If all went well, they'd venture off somewhere far from the uncanny revelation that SaeKu had fucked up. Once comfortable in bed, SaeKu gave God his praises and drifted into a slumber.

Chapter Three

Flat on his back, Dade listened to the soft snoring of Alani. Rolling over onto his side, he watched as her chest rose and then fell. Everything inside of him wished that it was SaeKu, sound asleep while he rested well. Exhaling, he turned back, tucking his arms under his head. The darkness made way for his thoughts, causing him to give into the desire that he'd been feeling to hold SaeKu near.

For the last two days, he'd been trying to get in a word with her, but she wasn't having it. His calls went unanswered, and his texts received no response. He was growing frustrated with her antics, but he understood her reasoning. Dade was floored by the amount of pain he must've been equipping SaeKu with.

With knowing that SaeKu would be leaving the island the very next day, Dade's desire to reach out to her outweighed any other source of emotion that was currently on his heart. Easing from the bed, he slid on a pair of Nike slides, and pulled a tee shirt over his abdomen. Sliding back the doors to the cabana, he was sure to keep quiet.

As Dade's walk of shame commenced, the sounds of the waves calmed his nervousness. A few feet away from his dwelling was SaeKu's. The lights were out, signaling that she was probably asleep. Lifting his hand, Dade knocked on the door repeatedly. After waiting and knocking for over five minutes, he realized that she wasn't going to answer, more than likely.

"SaeKu." He said to himself. "Open this fucking door, girl."

"Well, that sure wouldn't get you in." he heard from behind.

SaeKu was trailed by the rest of the girls. Each had a drink in their hand and a wobble in their step. Obviously, they'd been out having a good time. Dade chuckled at the fact that they didn't bother inviting Alani. The tolerance for her presence was at an all time low, and it was obvious, too. Giggles could be heard as they all dispensed to their appropriate settlements. Seconds passed, and the two were standing alone. Sage was the last to trail off, after double checking that her friend could handle her own.

"I'm fine." SaeKu nodded.

"Which goes without saying." Dade threw out.

"Furthermore, I wasn't going to answer the door if I was inside." SaeKu sipped her drink, and titled her head to the side. "Now, can you move so that I can make my way inside."

"SaeKu, we need to talk."

"No, Dade. We don't." SaeKu pushed Dade aside, and used the key to unlock the door.

Before she could grab the handle to slide the door open, her drink was tossed into the sand, and she was shoved forward. The door in front of her opened, and her body was pushed inside. With his hands gripping her scalp, Dade spun SaeKu around, and stared into her eyes.

"Yes the fuck we do, SaeKu." He leaned down and found the first source of pleasure, her lips. "Stop being so difficult," he detached himself from her juicy melons and gave her the once over.

After her insides stopped fuming with lust, it burned from anger. "Go!" SaeKu pushed Dade forward. "Just go!" she called again, shoving him harder the second time. "How could you just…" she stared, but couldn't bare the thought of the words she wanted to say actually coming from her lips.

"I'm not going anywhere. SaeKu." Dade called with his arms wide stretched. "I fucked up."

"You're right, Dade. You're right about that. Now, please." She cried. "Just leave." With her hand pointed towards the door, she insisted that he went away. Unsteadily, her fingers shook, violently, displaying the uncontrollable emotions that were fighting to see the light.

The tears splashed onto the floor beneath her. Although the droplets splattered and were silent in nature, the reasoning behind their existence was more impactful then one could imagine. Each tear that tumbled down SaeKu's face and to the ground was like a small grenade being dropped onto Dade's heart. Quick on his feet, he pulled SaeKu in for a hug, and demanded that she heard his cry, too.

"I waited for you, SaeKu. I waited. I'm still waiting. Nothing has changed. This situation could be history if you told me that with me is where you want to be. I know this is all fucked up, and I wish that I would've ran into you before this shit got this deep. I fault nobody but myself. I should've searched for you a bit harder, or fought until you gave in. I just wanted to give you time, but you took too much of that shit." Dade gritted his teeth. "I'm sorry." He finished off, lifting her head so that she could look into his eyes and witness the pain and regret that he was experiencing.

"You…" SaeKu's back lifted before falling. Over and over, she blinked away her tears. "You broke it." She admitted what she'd been avoiding. "You broke my heart, Dade."

"And I'm sorry, mama. I swear to God that I am. I know this shit isn't easy to handle, but it's not what you think, SaeKu." Dade gave into the possibility of Alani's child not being his.

"You told me you'd wait, Dade." SaeKu reminded him.

"I have yet to break that promise SaeKu." Dade claimed. "I can prove that shit to you if this is what you really want."

Dade could take no more. Impulsive by nature, he threw all cautions to the wind, and tried his hand. Curing the pain, he'd caused with sexual pleasures would only last so long, but at least it would sooth for the moment. Afterward, he'd work out the kinks. As of now, temporary relief sounding like a good idea. He was willing to try anything in the sake of helping SaeKu's feelings subside.

Starting at her forehead, Dade landed tender kisses. Next, he kissed the tears from her lids. SaeKu continued to weep as Dade found her lips, and gave them an extra bit of attention. Then it was her chin and each side of her neck. SaeKu's anger dissipated with each stroke of his lips.

It was amazing how a man could be the source of your pain, yet the only solution. The very person that knocked you down, was the only one that could pick you up. Although he'd broken it, all she wanted was for him to fix whatever it was. A woman's cries and pleas were calls for clarity and the repairing of the heart. Not often did they wish for separation or dejection of status, but more so the uplifting of a spirit bruised and beat down.

This man was her epidemic, and her remedy. He'd caused soreness all over, but his compassion filled touches were soothing the aching in both her mind and heart. Had he walked out of the door, as SaeKu had demanded, the discomfort would've been much too much to bare. It was the strangest force of nature that kept her yarning his presence, but wishing for his absence.

Wanting to listen to the alarms sounding off in her head, SaeKu begged for the strength to disengage from sexual activities, knowing that disappointment would come after. However, her heart spoke louder and its message was clearer. Like many other women, she chose the ladder. The heart wanted what the heart wanted, and following feelings were much easier than battling thoughts. Thoughts required too much, when feelings came quite natural.

The dispensing off ill feelings commenced as her assailant combed over her body with kisses, equipped with promises to nurture her soul –even if only for a night. Falling victim to his web, once again, SaeKu spun out of control with a hollowing gasp from her tongue. He'd reached her honey pot, sucking her sensitive bulb into the same set of lips that had graced her forehead, eyelids, nose, mouth, neck, chin, and breast.

Ashamed that her body and heart had ganged up on her mind, leaving it no choice but to surrender, SaeKu desperately tried muffling her moans. The urge to scream out became too intense as she felt her body being lifted from it's natural state to a place much more whimsical. Self-satisfaction had driven her to this cliff many nights that she'd spent alone. However, riding passenger as Dade steered was much more enjoyable and gratifying.

**

Dade woke to the early morning glow. His head was still spinning from the love making that he and SaeKu had indulged in the previous night. While Alani was the last thing on his mind last night, he knew that she was probably worried sick waking up to an empty bed. Shrugging his shoulders, Dade rolled over to start the morning off with a bit more moaning before making his way back over to his place.

His forehead wrinkled with confusion as his body fell forward, hitting the mattress. Sitting up in bed, Dade yelled out. "SaeKu!" he called.

A few seconds passed, and he wasn't granted a response. Flipping the covers back, his eyes darted towards the corner of the room where her suitcase had been. He'd only known it was there because he nearly took his toe off in the dark because of it. Running his hand over his face, he summed up the reasoning behind the missing luggage. SaeKu had departed.

"FUCK!" Dade grabbed at his curly tresses.

Throwing the cover back, he pulled himself from the bed, and gathered his clothing. Chuckling on the way out of the door, he thought of how slick SaeKu thought she was. However, he had something for that ass. There were two more days left in paradise, and then it was back to the jungle to hunt her ass down like a lion's prey. She wouldn't stand a chance this time. He'd comb each corner of the melting pot until he stumbled upon his girl.

Sliding the door of SaeKu's place closed, Dade turned with a smile plastered on his lips. It, quickly, fell into the sand as he made eye contact with Alani. She was simply breathtaking in her long cover up, and one-piece swimwear. His words were caught in his throat as he admired her pregnancy glow, but cringed at the chaotic look that was smeared on her face.

"Really Dade?" Alani folded her arms over her chest, and waited for a response.

"Give me a minute, and I promise I'll be ready to roll."

Dade avoided her question, and made his way to their place. Once inside, he stripped out of his clothing, and took a five-minute shower. While inside, thoughts of SaeKu lingered. Her deep chocolate skin resting against his chest and her pink pouty lips puckering up for deep kisses. Everything about that girl drove him wild, and he couldn't wait to finally have her in his life. Although he hated that Alani's presence had, basically, destroyed SaeKu, it was helpful. In his mind, she wouldn't have ever opened up to him hadn't she witnessed another woman playing her roll.

The days to follow seemed to linger, antagonizing Dade. He was counting down the hours until he got back to the city. Luckily, within 48 hours, he was walking through the airport doors, looking around for their ride back home.

"Over here, nigga." Lorde yelled, pulling a blunt from his lips. His head was poking out of the roof of his ride. Smoke traveled through the air in huge clouds, causing Dade to shake his head.

"We're on federal property, and you chiefin."

"A nigga has had a very fucked up day. Not you or the federal dick heads can stop me from taking this much needed blunt to the head." Lorde pulled off. Dade had tossed their bags into the trunk, and gotten into the backseat, allowing Alani to grab the passenger seat.

"Here." Lorde tried handing the blunt to Dade, but he declined. "Trust me. You may want to hit this for what I'm about to tell you."

Dade's muscles tensed, and he pulled the blunt between his thumb and index finger. Silence struck the air like lightening during a thunderous storm. Lorde's hesitation rubbed Dade the wrong way. Figuring whatever he had to say would be unpleasing, he decided to go ahead and get it over with.

"What's the news?"

"Mama. They're keeping her this time."

Clinching his fist, Dade silently cursed under his breath. "FUCK!" he gritted.

"How long?" he asked.

"30 days top." Lorde broke the news. Just yesterday, he'd rushed his mother to the emergency room. Neither of them knew that her stomach pains were a result corroding –in which her cancer was causing. Her body was becoming weaker by the day, and the thought of losing her was eating away at her boys.

"Oh my God." Alani's hands covered her mouth as she started to weep.

Looking over in her direction, Lorde shook his head. "She don't even fuck with you, though. Why you crying and shit? What's wrong?"

"Lorde." Dade felt awful about the amount of amusement he discovered in Lorde's words. This was a serious matter, and he was being his normal self. As fucked up as he was, he always kept it one-hundred.

"What, nigga? I'm just saying."

"Take Alani home." Dade waved Lorde's foolishness off, and changed the subject.

"I was headed that way." Lorde assured Dade.

There was no way that he was taking Alani anywhere near his mother. Lauren did not like her or Gia. She felt as if they both had ulterior motives. Lorde didn't see any concerns when it came to Alani, but Gia was the definition of a shiesty bitch. You couldn't trust her as far as you could see her.

Alani hadn't paid much attention to the direction they were headed in. However, her face burned when she realized she'd been brought to her condo. "Why are we here?" she questioned.

"He said bring you home, so I brought you home."

"I doubt if he meant here. I'm certain he meant the home that we share together."

"Oh, his home? Dade, my bad. You have to be more specific next time." Lorde shrugged.

"Baby, let me help you out. I'll be back soon to get you. I need to go check on my aunt, and then I'll be back." Dade soothed her burning soul, as he exited the car. Once inside of her place, Dade kissed Alani goodbyes, and headed back out. He'd arranged her bags inside of her closet, and given her some cash to busy herself while he was away.

"Let me see your phone." Dade stretched his hand out when he hopped back in the car. "With your foul ass. Why you always clowning her?"

"I'm not. I just know that she's wasting her time, homie. So are you. I can almost bet you're using my phone to call ole girl. She blocked that ass, huh?" Lorde called his bluff.

"Don't worry about me, nigga." Dade countered. "Just let me see your jack."

Lorde reached in his pocket and handed Dade his cell. Dade scrolled through his contacts until he stumbled upon SaeKu's number. He'd been calling, but wasn't able to reach her. Now that Lorde mentioned it, he figured that she had blocked him. The thought stung a bit.

Dade input SaeKu's digits into Lorde's cell, and waited for an answer. On the third ring, her angelic tone tickled Dade's ears. His chest swelled and his heart rate sped up a bit. There was no one in the world who had ever had such an effect on him. It was evident that SaeKu was needed to supply his high, but so much had gotten in the way of them that Dade wondered if they could ever really be.

"Hello." She sung like a sweet melody.

"I need you." Dade was honest, too afraid that she'd hang up on him if he wasn't straight forward.

"Send me a location." SaeKu ended the call and lifted her head from the firm pillow.

She'd just completed another assignment, and would be on her way home in a few. Dade's call was perfect timing. She was searching for the will to get up after exhaustion swept over her like a wave.

Three hours and a few minutes elapsed before SaeKu was stepping onto the elevator, and heading up to the floor that Dade's aunt was housed on. She had no clue what she was stepping into, but the distress that was present in Dade's voice when he reached out was enough to get her to where she needed to be in order to assist him. Still dressed in uniform, her navy blue attire hugged her small frame as her heels connected with the floor each time she stepped.

Upon entering the ICU's waiting room, SaeKu was struck by the pure beauty of a creature so well defined that she nearly lost her balance. Whereas she was accustomed to Dade exuding power and strength, she'd been introduced to the diminished version of the man that she'd grown to fall in love with. His burdens weighed heavy on her, already, broken heart, immediately. Dade's energy transferred to her, bringing tears to her eyes. He had yet to state his case, but SaeKu had passed judgment, instantaneously. Her baby was hurting.

"Dade." She called out, rushing to his side.

His fingers had been entangled in his curly locs of silk as he lifted his head. The worry shined, sitting at the center of his pupils. A heavy sigh met his lips as he stood and stretched his arms to pull SaeKu into them.

Inhaling, SaeKu demanded that his presence overtake her. His cologne, his body, his sensual touches, his kisses, and his caress all meant something to her. They made an irresistible combination that would soften the toughest of women.

"What's the matter," she raked his chin into her hands, cupping it. She forced him to look into her eyes and speak his peace.

Instead of speaking, Dade grabbed the back of SaeKu's head, and brought her face near. He rested his lips on her luscious set, and inhaled her womanly fragrance. She meant the world to him, and if it was his to give then she could have it. Pulling back, he looked into her tearful eyes. It was no secret that she was silently mourning the lost of whatever they could've had. It tore Dade to pieces that he even had to continue to subject her to the realization of it, but his selfishness just wouldn't allow her to bow out in peace. He wanted her. He needed her.

"I have someone I want you to meet." Dade cleared his throat and grabbed SaeKu by the hand. She trailed him down the hallway, one that was quiet enough to hear a pin drop. Her heels were causing a ruckus as they treaded.

Dade pushed the door to the eighth room that they passed open, and ushered SaeKu inside. He gave her no prior warning of what she was about to walk into. She saddened at the sight of a frail woman, looking to only be in her forties. Her skin was pale and her hair was piled on top of her head.

"SaeKu, this is my mom, Lauren." Dade startled her with his words. She'd gotten so lost in her thoughts that she'd forgotten that he was standing behind her.

"Aunt." Lauren cleared her throat and opened her eyes. She'd been resting, barely. When she heard Dade speak, she willed herself to consciousness.

"This is my mother, Lauren. Mom, this is SaeKu. I've mentioned her to you before."

"Several times. Hell, I was tired of you talking about the damn girl. I'm glad to see you really exist, because I thought he was speaking of a ghost. I had started not to believe the hype, but you are as beautiful as he described." Lauren's muscles ached, but she conjured up a smile anyhow.

"Well, it's nice to know that Dade had great things to say about me. It's nice meeting you!" SaeKu inched closer to the bed. "How are you feeling?"

"Like a woman that's dying, I suppose." Lauren shrugged.

"MA!" Lorde called out.

SaeKu's eyes darted towards the corner that the sound had emerged. She hadn't noticed anyone else was in the room.

"Chill out."

"Well, it's the truth, son."

"Anyway. I feel pretty decent, considering the circumstances." She cut her eyes towards Lorde. "That's my son, Lorde. Lord bless his soul." SaeKu had no clue what Lauren meant, but she was sure to find out soon.

"Nice to meet you." SaeKu nodded.

"You know how to do a little hair?" Lauren asked.

"I can do a little something." SaeKu nodded, sitting her purse on the table next to the bed. "What you trying to get?"

"Something." Lauren shrugged. "Anything but this mess. I can imagine how crazy I look laying up here. These two boys aren't any help at all."

Lorde's eyes bulged out of his sockets. He couldn't believe that his mother had taken so well to SaeKu, immediately. She was hard on everyone that they'd ever introduced her to. Lorde wondered if the cancer had begun to work on her brain cells as well, because she couldn't have been thinking clearly. His mother was a tough cookie, and she opened right up to SaeKu.

A huge weight was lifted off of Dade's shoulders. SaeKu was fragile, and he would've been no more good had Lauren not accepted her. In a way, this was confirmation that he needed to do whatever it took to win her over. In his mind, she was it for him. The minute he cleaned up the mess he'd made, he would give her whatever her little heart desired. The thought alone had him anxious, wishing that he could just speed up time. However, looking at his mother in her current state, he knew that with time fast-forwarded, it would mean the death of her. That was just something Dade wasn't willing to accept at the moment.

"Take me off block." Dade said before getting deep into conversation with SaeKu. They had spent hours at the hospital with his mom. He'd even made a few runs and come back to SaeKu still at Lauren's bedside.

"I can't do that, Dade." SaeKu sighed. "And you know that."

"Why not?" Dade questioned.

"Because this is the only way I can make this happen."

"Make what happen?" Dade frowned.

"Me getting over you. It's the only way." She admitted. "You having access to me is not going to help."

"Keeping me on block isn't either. Why would you even try to get over me? If fighting this thing is so much of a task, then it's probably because it's the wrong thing to do. Why sweat a nigga? You know this is what you want, too."

"Dade, you have a lot going on, right now."

"A lot that I'm ready to kiss good-bye."

"You have a child on the way for Christ's sake." SaeKu yelled.

"The possibilities of that are slim to none." Dade shrugged. "I doubt if Alani's child is mine."

"Then why are you there?"

"Because I'm a man, that's why."

"Dade…" SaeKu started.

"But let's not talk about that, SaeKu."

"How can we not? It's the only thing that I've been having for breakfast, lunch, and dinner. It's the only thing in my dreams. It greets me in the morning when I open my eyes, and haunts me in my sleep while they're shut. How can we not talk about it, huh?" SaeKu was crushed at the thought of Dade fathering a child that weren't made between the two of them.

"That lady up there told me something when you left out. She told me to stop at nothing, and I have to honor her word." Dade grabbed SaeKu's hand and placed it at his chest.

"That thing right there." He referred to his heart. "It longs for you. It waits for you. It beats for you." He preached, hoping to get through to her. "Give me some time to fix this."

"Dade…"

"Shhhh… In the meantime, allow me to treat you to dinner. Let me make up for every meal your body has been deprived of because of my foolishness. Please."

“I don’t know if that’s a good idea.”

“Listen. I’m telling you tonight that my decision has been made. I’m done chasing you, SaeKu. This was meant, and I’m going to go to my grave seeing it through.”

“I just don’t know.”

“Yeah you do.” He rebutted. “Where do you want to go? Chose anywhere in the world, and I’ll see to it that we get there.”

“Let me think about it.”

**

“Bitch, don’t be crazy.” Sage rolled her eyes as she blew the polish on her nails. Their cozy two-bedroom apartment was stationed in the heart of the Bronx. Loud horns and motorist could be heard throughout the day, and drunks walking the streets at night.

“I’m saying, Sage. He has a baby on the way.”

“He said the damn baby isn’t his. You going to make the baby be his, SaeKu?”

“No, but he didn’t exactly say that.”

“Well, you asked my opinion, so I told you. I say go for it. If you find out otherwise, then drop it.” Sage shrugged. “Has he ever had a reason to lie to you?”

“No.”

“Good, then. Take his word.”

“I don’t want to end up getting hurt, Sage. We both know how this works. Once she has the baby, if it’s his… their connection will be stronger and shit between us will slowly dwindle. I don’t know if I can handle all of that.”

"You're thinking too much."

"I'm not thinking enough." SaeKu mumbled, falling back onto the couch. Her mind was in a fog. She desperately needed fresh air to clear some mental space. Lifting back up, she grabbed her keys and headed out of the door.

As SaeKu pulled the door open, she was greeted by the familiar smell of intoxication. Looking up, she came into contact with Dade. It had been over 24 hours since they'd last seen each other. His presence made her wonder why the thought of missing him hadn't crossed her mind. Now that he was standing before her, she realized just how much she did.

"How did you get up here?"

"Money talk bullshit walk." Dade shrugged.

"I'll be sure to have the security fired."

"It's been a whole day." Dade dodged the subject, moving on to a more important one.

"How did you even know where to find me?"

"Are we going to play 21 questions, or are you going to be woman enough to answer the one I asked an entire day ago."

"How is your mom?"

"She's holding on." Dade softened at the thought of Lauren. "SaeKu, are you going to answer my question. Shit, or take a nigga off the block list."

"I was thinking, and I still don't think either is a good idea." SaeKu stuffed her hands in her pockets to remove the residue from her sweaty palms.

"I see." Dade chuckled. Grabbing SaeKu by the neck, he pinned her to the front door of her apartment, causing a thud. "A nigga got to get physical for you to feel what he's saying. Well, SaeKu, I'm going to give you what you want." He whispered in her ear.

Twirling the knob to her door, he pushed it open, and shoved her inside. Sage jumped up, alarmed with thoughts of danger. After realizing it was Dade, she wore a smile bigger than paid actors for Colgate commercials. She watched as Dade handled SaeKu wtih little to no force, betting that her roommate would have to hang her panties out to dry once Dade was done with her.

Dade grabbed the back of SaeKu's neck, and pulled her into his chest. "I swear I don't get you." He whispered. "You got me showing out in front of your people and shit."

"That's all you." SaeKu countered.

"Where's your room?" he asked. SaeKu refused to say a word, so Sage spoke up.

"Last door to the right. Not the left, because that's mine."

Dade followed the trail that lead to the hallway, and then to SaeKu's bedroom. It was cozy, and girly, just as he imagined. Closing the door behind them, Dade released SaeKu from his grasp. He'd barely been using any force to restrain her, which let him know that she was appreciative of a little roughness.

"Why you playing with a nigga? Huh? Fuck you want me to do, get on my knees and beg your ass to go out on a date? Huh? Because that shit ain't going to happen. I'll tell you what is, though. You're about to bend that ass over the bed, and I'm going to give you my best shit. Once we're both in the moment, I'm going to demand that you go on that date with me. You'll be so fucking wrapped up into this good dick that I have to give that you'll agree to a threesome if I asked. Afterwards, I'm going to doze off, because a nigga is tired as fuck. I'm going to wake up to you beside me, and we're going to decide where we're going for our date. We both know that pillow talk has you feeling like you can conquer the world the next day. Do we have an understanding?"

While Dade spoke to SaeKu, he removed articles of clothing. By the time he was done, he'd removed each layer, and was massaging his muscle while waiting for her to do the same. Staring into his handsome face, SaeKu sighed, realizing she was going to do everything he had just said. Her eyes traveled the length of his body, and then met back up with his erection. The enticing vein stretched for miles, or so it seemed.

"Take that shit off." He demanded. "And then come get right here… on your knees." Dade was forceful with his words, causing SaeKu to practice compliance.

Chapter Four

Dressed in a pair of denim and an oversized t-shirt, SaeKu strutted through the the galleria, with Sage at her side. Together, the two were a force to be reckoned with. Women nearly caught cataract from rolling their contacts into their heads at the sight of the two, and men were no better. They flocked to the pair like bees to honey.

"Are you sure that's all?" SaeKu questioned Sage.

"Yes. I promise." Sage giggled. "That's it, yo!" Her New York accent shined, brightly.

"Good. I have a few hours to make the spa and get dressed."

SaeKu had decided to take Dade up on his date offer, and was all nerves. The two had known one another for as far back as SaeKu could remember, so her nervousness was baffling in a sense. She'd been on edge all morning and well throughout the evening.

As Dade had revealed, they made passionate love well into the night. SaeKu was reluctant to rest her worries on his bare chest as they're heartbeats matched and breathing aligned. It was as if their bodies were in sync. The two shells fit perfectly as their spirits entangled, wrapping one another deeper into the web that had been spun.

"And take a nap. You forgot to add that." Sage teased. "I don't even think you guys got a wink last night. If it wasn't moaning and growling that I heard on both of your ends, then it was whispers."

"Hush, chile!" SaeKu pushed Sage through the automatic doors as they exited the shopping center.

"You know I'm not lying. I'm happy for you, Sae." Sage pumped her fist into the air. "SaeKu been getting the D all week."

"Shut up!" SaeKu's skin turned purple.

"Now, if I could just get me a little something something. Does Dade have like… a twin brother? One that's just like him? A little more hood? Like to talk shit? Prefers someone that's completely opposite of him? Like to blow a bank? And can have my ass running up the walls trying to go home to God when we're in the bedroom?"

"Oh my God. You're awful. What am I going to do with you?" SaeKu was in tears, leaning over while trying to get a handle on her laughing.

"What? I'm serious. I can do without the hood, but I love a man that's a product of his environment. You know… One with the origin, but has progressed in a major way. Like a gentlethug."

"What the hell is a gentlethug?"

"A thug turned gentleman." Sage shrugged.

"Are you serious, right now?"

"Yes. Those do exist, you know?"

“Sage. Please. Let’s just get out of here before you give me a heart attack.” SaeKu pulled Sage’s arm.

As the girls journeyed to the nailshop, SaeKu kept stilling glances at Sage. She’d become silent, which was highly unlike her. She was a blabber mouth, and silence just wasn’t her forte. Her nose was stuck in her phone, as a stoned expression crossed her beautiful brown colored skin.

“What’s up? You good?”

“Today is their anniversary.” Sage sighed.

“We can detour.” SaeKu insisted.

“No, it’s fine. I will spend time with them on tomorrow. I was going out there, anyway. They need new flowers.”

Sage’s parents had been snatched from her life at the tender age of eleven. She’d gone to school with an attitude because she wanted pink hair like her privileged Caucasian friends. Her parents weren’t having it, so she’d grew angrier with them by the day.

Unbeknownst to Sage, her mother had called around to every beauty supply in their vicinity and stumbled across one with temporary hair colorant. After a few days, the box instructions said that it would wash right out.

Her mother was a housewife, and had never worked a day in her life. The love birds had met when they were teenagers, and their union blossomed as time progressed. Aubrey, Sage’s mother was at her father’s workplace each day to bring him lunch. That day was no different.

However, they spent his lunch break at the beauty supply, buying every color temporary dye that they had on the shelf so that their precious Sage would end her strike against them.

Unfortunately, on the way back to her father's job, they crossed paths with an 18-wheeler, driven by a man who suffered a massive heart attack behind the wheel and died. His truck spun out of control. The truck rear ended her parents, and the impact caused their small Mercedes to flee from the road.

Sage could remember the day that her principle walked into her classroom and pulled her out. The news of her parent's fatal car crash broke her spirit. She became a timid young girl. Fostered by less then appealing blood relatives, her lifestyle was stripped from her. She could barely handle the stress that seven years of misfortunes had caused. Sage passed time by planning for the day that she became a woman.

On her eighteenth birthday, the caged bird was set free at last. Her inheritance was accessible, immediately. Being that she'd planned, strategically, for that day to come, Sage didn't go and blow a check. She'd chosen everything from the apartment that she wanted to the bathroom set that target had on sale. Within four days, her little place was furnished and she had moved in. From that day on, Sage had been granted her happiness. She was no longer the timid little eleven-year-old. Sage was as bright as a shooting star, and SaeKu loved every ounce of her.

"You sure?" SaeKu questioned.

"Yeah. There's a spot." Sage lifted her head just in time to see someone pulling out of their parking spot.

"Oh goody. We're right in front."

"Come on. I know they are about to get their evening rush."

"Nigga, you can have this bitch. All I'm saying is watch where you lay them hands. This bitch doesn't belong to me. She belongs to the streets, but that precious being she's carrying is all me." SaeKu and Sage strained their necks trying to find the source.

"I'm a grown ass man, dog. Can't no nigga tell me where to lay my hands. Furthermore, you should be careful of what you claim." SaeKu and Sage were finally able to locate the confrontation. To the left of them stood a pregnant woman who stood beside a dark skinned man. In front of them was a familiar face, one that SaeKu couldn't forget if she tried.

"You running your cocksucker like you're telling me some shit I don't know. Gia, you stuck on stupid while this nigga thinking he snitching. Keep talking, my G, and I'm going to knock the gravy out your biscuit."

"What the hell is going on?"

"Ssssshhhh." SaeKu placed her hand over her mouth. She didn't want to get caught snooping.

"Now we throwing threats?" the young man laughed, obviously pissing Lorde off.

Without another word passed between the two of them, Lorde pulled out his piece, and cocked it.

"LORDE!" SaeKu stepped from behind her car.

SaeKu could no longer contain her presence. She did not want to see Lorde being hauled away in a police car because he reacted impulsively to a hood reject. Although she didn't know him, she knew the struggle that was within. His anger was at an all time high. His mother was dying, and there wasn't anything he could do to save her.

Whoever the guy was that he was about to off wasn't worth the heartache that his mother would be subjected to just before death. It was obvious that the young man was envious. Not only was it in his demeanor, but his eyes as well. SaeKu was a great judge of character, and she knew that he was a bunch of fluff. In actuality, he was scared of the harm Lorde could cause. He hid it with the back talk and mean glares.

Lorde kept his eyes trained on his victim. "What's up SaeKu?" he spoke as if the two had known each other for a lifetime. He remembered her voice. There was no need to turn to view her stance, he knew the angelic soul was frightened by his aggressiveness.

He never missed a beat as he continued. "It's a blessing that I don't want to run my sister-in-law off, being that my brother has finally gotten a grip on her ass." He bashed the young man in the head with his pistol. "Otherwise… that was your ass." He struck him, again. This time, he knocked the guy to the ground. Lorde stood over his body, and then kneeled beside him.

Looking up at SaeKu, he asked. "You ready for that nigga to take you on a date? He at the barbershop getting all pretty for you, now." Lorde informed SaeKu as she stood in shock. She couldn't understand why her feet wouldn't move, even though she knew that she needed to get out of dodge.

"That nigga head over heels for you." Lorde spread the young guy's hands over his head. He was barely conscious as Lorde bashed his gun onto his right hand, then did the same to the left.

WHAM.

"AHHH!" You could hear screams and groans from the guys mouth.

WHAM.

WHAM.

WHAM.

Blood splattered onto the concrete. The spectators had concluded the fact that he wouldn't be able to use either hand after Lorde was finished with him. Over and over, he punctured his hands with the butt of his gun. "Don't ever mention my name and threat in the same sentence, bitch. Let that be a lesson. Next time I say watch your hands, nigga... WATCH YOUR MOTHERFUCKING HANDS. You could've agreed and kept this shit one-hundred."

Lorde huffed and puffed. "Got me out here fucking up the knees of my $1,000 jeans. Matter of fact." Lorde paused. Placing his gun at his waist, Lorde dug his hand into the pockets of the guy he'd just violated. He pulled out a small knot and chuckled.

"You falling off." He looked up to Gia. "This nigga got a big bank full of ones. Fuck he was taking you to lunch at, Burger King? I can't even replace my jeans with this shit."

Lifting up, Lorde pocketed the money and walked over towards Gia. With a smile on his face, he bent down and kissed her belly. "Don't be feeding my baby that fucking dog food." He hissed before turning off. "Y'all need anything?"

"Some money." Gia rolled her eyes while rubbing her stomach.

"Here." Lorde removed his personal bank, and handed it to Gia. Unlike ole boy, his shit was laced with hundreds and fifties. "And pick a better fuck buddy next time. I do not approve of that fuck nigga."

"Whatever Lorde. You need to stay out of my business."

"I will… As soon as you drop that load, you can fuck the sewer cleaner for all I give a fuck."

"I can't stand you, nigga." Gia rolled her eyes.

"The feelings are mutual baby mama." Lorde said, sarcastically.

"Real funny. You ain't have to say it like that." Gia frowned.

"You know what's up. That's all you are, and that's all you'll ever be. You round here fucking fresh bums and shit. You're due any day, now, Gia. It would make sense to be somewhere relaxing." Lorde scoffed.

He couldn't believe that he'd once worshiped the ground that Gia walked on. It hadn't even been a year since their split, and she was showing her true colors. She'd pinned a child on him, and he'd stopped hitting her raw after they separated. However, he was willing to play her games if that mean him having his princess in return.

"Fuck you Lorde."

"Na, shawty. That pussy dead weight. You might as well throw that bitch away. I hate my daughter even has to come through that motherfucker." Lorde laughed.

"You foul, nigga."

"I learned from you."

Lorde had lost all respect for Gia the day that she was caught on tape sucking dick behind a dumpster. Crazy thing is, they were still together. After he was passed the footage, he barged in his home and put her out on her ass. Two months later, she was pregnant. Lorde was open to the thought of the baby being his until they found out exactly how far along she was.

Once the results came back, he calculated the dates –being that he was great at numbers. It didn't add up, but he didn't mention it. Lorde had become too attached to the thought of having a little one, especially with his mother's condition. His little one would love him, unconditionally. That's exactly what he needed.

Gia stormed off, throwing up the middle finger. "See you soon, Gia." Lorde called out.

"My bad about that." Lorde turned to SaeKu. "I-"

Bzzzzzzz. Bzzzzzz.

The ringing of a phone caused Lorde to pat the pockets of his jeans. He pulled out an iPhone, but stuffed it back inside of his pocket. Reaching into the other pocket, he pulled out two flips phones, and stuffed one back inside of his jeans. The other, he flipped open, and pressed to his ear. He began to walk off, but stopped in front of Sage.

"You been standing your fine ass over here this whole time and ain't say shit? You were going to let me send that nigga to his maker, and miss this opportunity. Shame on you. I hope you was ready to foot a nigga's commissary. You ever held a nigga down before?" Lorde questioned.

Before Sage could form a sentence, another phone of his rang out loud. Her eyes widened as he pulled the iPhone from his jeans, again. "I'm on my way." He said. "Duty calls, but I'll see you around." he nodded, jogging backwards. Sage watched as he jumped into a silver G-Wagon, bumping Trap or Die 3.

"Who in the shit was that?" Sage sang dramatically. Her heart pumped like an unborn child. Her lids hung low in lust, and the panties could use a clean up.

"Nobody you need to worry about. That boy would mess up your life."

"I could use a fucked up life right now." Sage threw all caution out of the window.

"SAGE!" SaeKu laughed. "Listen to yourself."

"You're probably right. A little chaos is good sometimes, though, right?" Sage asked. SaeKu ignored her question, shaking her head.

"Just…" was the only word that came to mind.

"Here. Please take this. I need to get these panties off so that I can hang them out to dry." Sage tried handing her purse over to SaeKu.

"Forgive me, mama, but I think I just fell in love with a thug." Sage looked to the sky.

"Come on crazy!"

Sage was completely hypnotized by the handsome thug with the bald head. Everything about him made her ooze at the center. She wanted to know more about this guy, but she'd never tell a soul –other than her bestie. The two went on about their day, but thoughts of Lorde lingered much long after his departure.

Sage heard everything that SaeKu had said, but she wanted to see what was really good with the project poster kid. All she'd known her entire life was corporate thugs. When she met the crew from Philly, she was smitten by their high class hood mentality. Now, she craved a piece of the pie.

**

Armani covered Dade from head to toe. He was dapper in the heather grey attire. His curls had been shampooed and tamed to suit the occasion. He'd pulled out every stop to see that beautiful smile on SaeKu's face. Dade couldn't remember a time when he'd put any amount of effort or planning into one night. SaeKu was special, though. He knew it, and everyone around them did as well.

KNOCK.

KNOCK.

His knuckles hit the solid wood on the yellow door. SaeKu and Sage had painted it nearly a year ago, simply because they wanted to take the edge off of the boring brown color that it was originally.

SaeKu appeared behind the door with happiness in high pursue. Her chocolate beauty was bone chilling. The satin romper and trench hugged her small frame, pinpointing her curves. Her hair was in a sleek bob with a blunt cut, and a platinum blonde highlight on the tip of her right side bang.

"Well." Dade was at a loss for words. With time, SaeKu had grown to be more gorgeous, and Dade had once doubted if that was even possible. "Um."

"I'm ready." SaeKu acknowledged the fact that she'd kept her promise. Dade had begged her not to keep him waiting too long, and she'd fallen through.

"I see." Dade complimented. "You look amazing."

"Thanks babe." SaeKu smiled. "Are these for me?"

"Yeah." Dade handed SaeKu the bouquet of freshly picked roses.

"Thanks." She inhaled. "Let me sit these down, and I will be right back."

SaeKu went back inside of the house, and Dade's eyes followed her every move until she disappeared. He picked at his goatee as he awaited her return, thinking of all the things he wanted to do to her before the night was out.

"Ready?"

"Always."

SaeKu looped her arm inside of Dade's and they both walked down the hall. Once outside, SaeKu felt the effects of the night air. Her hair blew, slightly with the wind, and her satin attire followed suit.

"You know… You look nice, yourself."

"You buggin."

"I'm serious. Really. You look damn good, in fact. Stand over there." SaeKu let go of Dade's arm and stood off to the side.

She admired his frame, snapping a picture with her phone. It wasn't often that a woman felt the need to compliment her man, and show him the same attention that he did when she was looking good. SaeKu was all about showering her significant other. That wasn't supposed to be a one-way street. She felt it necessary to fluff your mates tail, helping to cushion their inflated ego.

"Stop it." Dade blushed, rushing back to her side.

"I'm just saying. You're looking like a million bucks, tonight."

"A measly million?" Dade exclaimed. "I'm insulted."

"You get what I'm trying to say." SaeKu clung to Dade's arm as they approached his Mercedes.

He pulled the door open for her, then ran around to the driver side once she was tucked away. Within a matter of seconds, they were pulling off into traffic. As sophisticated as he looked, he pumped up the volume to some old school Boosie. The windows rattled, and the two of them rapped word for word together.

When, "Betrayed," had spun out, Dade cut down the volume and they both burst into laughter. "What you know about that?" He joked.

"Don't count me all the way out. I know a little something about Boosie." SaeKu blushed. "I loved that song."

"Yeah, he was spitting some real shit." Dade nodded, and then turned the music back up. He had to replay that one just because it was that damn real.

They arrived at their destination soon after leaving SaeKu's place. Their reservations were for eight, and they were five minutes ahead of time. Dade removed himself from the car, and then helped SaeKu out as well. They walked into the elegant space hand in hand.

"Livingston." Dade spoke to the host. "Reservations for Livingston."

"Right this way."

"This place doesn't even offer reservations." SaeKu whispered as they trailed the host.

"Rules only apply to ones wiling to follow them. Money talks. Bullshit walks." Dade pulled out SaeKu's chair when they approached their table. He'd reserved their table, and the three that were around them in order to have the amount of privacy that he thought they'd require.

"I've heard people rave about La Fàq, but I've never been inside."

"Well, you've been living under a rock. Their rave reviews aren't just because of it's prestige nature, but because they have damn good food. The cooks are black. I've met them all, personally."

"Really?"

"Really. After dinner, I can give you a tour of the place."

"We can't just walk around here like we own the place, silly. These people have work to do around here."

"But I do."

"Excuse me."

"Well, not entirely, but I own part of the place." Dade shrugged.

"Bullshit." SaeKu gasped.

"The owner ran into financial difficulties, and needed a loan. I considered it an investment. Instead of requiring him to pay the loan off, I had him offer me a seat at his table. I knew how much money this place was worth with the help of RaKeem. He worked his magic, and all else was history."

"So, the renovations that they had were…"

"All funded and overseen by Dade Livingston."

"Wow. That's amazing."

"So, enough about me. What's been going on with you?"

"Well, for starters, my dreams of Julliard are a no go. After getting over the devastation, I was offered a job with my best friend, Sage. I took the gig, which was becoming a flight attendant. Fast forward to now, and I'm working on rebranding a blog I started a while back. My life is pretty black and white… There aren't any shaded or gray areas. Work and home. Work and home. What about you?"

"Everything is the same for me. Ain't shit changed."

"Oh really? It seems as if that's…"

"That's not me."

Dade knew that the possibility of Alani's daughter being his was slim to none. There was only one incident that he recalled where she could have gotten pregnant, but he was almost certain that it wasn't the case. His mind often played tricks on his, fumbling with the idea of fathering a child, but he knew this couldn't be the route that he'd take into fatherhood.

"Dade, you don't have to lie to me. I've made it up in my mind that it's something that I can't change, and I need to just let go of all thoughts of us ever being anything than what we've become over the years –distant memories." SaeKu shrugged as the waitress appeared at their table with plates and bottles. SaeKu didn't understand, but she didn't complain. They had yet to order anything, but their food had come.

"That doesn't have to be the case. In fact, it won't be." Dade continued after the waitress had left. "I gave them a list of foods you'd probably like, so go ahead and dig in."

Dade grabbed a glass, and poured SaeKu's wine. "Like I was saying… That's not me SaeKu. That can't be my kid."

"But there's a possibility?"

"Not really."

"Why am I finding that hard to believe?"

"Well, believe it. Alani knows that, and I do, too."

"So why..."

SaeKu's conversation was cut short by the ringing of Dade's cell. "Sorry." He held his finger up, asking if he could have a second. He answered the phone, mumbled a few words, and then ended the call, abruptly.

"SaeKu. There's been an emergency. I need to get to the hospital." He scooted back in his chair, and stood. Running around to SaeKu's end, he helped her from her chair, before they fled from the restaurant.

"Are you going to be okay?" SaeKu questioned as Dade sped through traffic.

"Yeah. I'm sorry about..."

"Don't mention it. We can do this again some other time."

"Thanks for understanding." Dade was back in front of SaeKu's building within a matter of minutes. "I'll call you." He leaned over and kissed her cheek. He hadn't parked his car, so he allowed her to get out directly in front of her place. She hurried out, and shut the door behind her.

"I'll be waiting. Drive safely." SaeKu waved, stepping onto the concrete.

"Alright."

Chapter Five

"What are they saying?" Dade asked, stepping into the hospital room.

"It was a false alarm. I thought this little girl was ready to make her entrance." Alani rubbed her stomach.

"So everything is good, though?" Dade wanted to make sure that there were no further complications.

"Yes. I was having back contractions, but I'm not in labor. I haven't even dilated any. I was in pain, so I came on."

"Oh. Aight." Dade nodded. "I thought it was time."

"We have nine more weeks." Alani sighed. "Then, I'll be forty weeks."

"Motherfuckers say you carry a baby for nine months, but that sounds like ten to me."

"Same thing I said." Alani giggled.

"They keeping you, or you're good to go home?"

"I'm waiting on discharge papers. I'll be free to go in a second. Before you walked in I was trying to find the strength to put on my clothes." She admitted.

"Here." Dade grabbed her clothes from the chair. "Let me help you with that."

He assisted Alani with her clothing, and they waited for her discharge papers. Dade arranged for her car to be picked up, and he drove her to his home. When they got inside, the first thought on his mind was SaeKu. Her dark skin was stamped in his memory. She was breathtaking that night, and he hated to run out on her so sudden. When he got settled, the first call he'd make would be to her.

It didn't take long for Alani to fall asleep counting sheep. As Dade watched over her, he imagined it was SaeKu in his bed with a bulging belly. He knew that she'd make an excellent mother and wife, and he couldn't wait til the day that they both became his reality.

Shutting off the bedroom lights, Dade went downstairs into the kitchen to fix himself a snack. The minute his feet hit the bottom step, he was Facetiming SaeKu. It didn't matter to him that Alani was upstairs sleeping. He was beginning to resent her presence as a whole. The only reason she was at his home instead of hers was because he wanted to make sure that she was looked after. Alani hadn't been back at his place since the day they'd returned from their trip.

"Hey, is everything okay?" SaeKu answered.

"Yeah. Everything is good. What you doing?"

"I just got in bed. I'm working on this website, so that I can finally put my blog to good use."

"Sounds like you're busy."

"Not even a little bit. I'm thinking of hiring a web designer. I want an entirely new site." SaeKu huffed.

"What's the hold up, then?"

"I don't know. I guess I haven't really looked into it, yet."

"Well, if you want it, then you should. Once you know the tab, then I'll give you the money to pay."

"You don't have to…"

"But I am. You miss me, yet?"

"What do you think?"

"I'm not sure, that's why I asked."

"Yes. Where did you go?"

"Ummm…" Dade hesitated. "Alani called crying because she thought she was in labor." He admitted.

"And you ran out on our date to do what, exactly?" SaeKu was all ears as she rolled her neck. Dade cringed at the disappointed look on her face.

"SaeKu."

"No. Help me understand how you're professing the fact that this child isn't yours one minute, and running out on our date because of a labor scare the next."

"Let me explain."

"Yeah. Please do."

"I've been fucking with Alani for a little minute, now. You've come into the picture, and I'm breaking things off. I haven't, yet, but all of this will be nipped in the bud by this week's end. I promise."

"Wait… So… You've been… You know what…" SaeKu didn't bother responding. She ended their FaceTime, abruptly, and blocked Dade's number.

Dade tried over and over to connect with SaeKu on FaceTime, but he continued to get an unavailable signal. After a few minutes, he gave up. The minute Alani woke up, her ass had to go so that he could slide through SaeKu's crib. She had him fucked up. She would be flying out the next day, so he needed to catch her before she jetted to a far away place.

It was two in the morning when Dade's fist collided with the yellow wooden door. He, honestly, didn't give a damn what time it was. SaeKu had been on his shit list since she hung up on him, and she was going to have to see him about that. Over and over, he banged his fist on the door of SaeKu's apartment.

"What the fuck is your problem?" Sage snatched the door open, half asleep. "I have to be up in just a few hours to catch a fucking flight. Unless you're going to board the plan for me, then I suggest you go home."

"Chill the fuck out, big shit. Where is SaeKu," Dade pushed through their front door.

"SaeKu isn't here." Sage lied.

Dade's ears turned red and burned like a lighter had been placed to each of them at the sound of SaeKu not being home at two in the morning. He'd spoken to her a few hours earlier, and she had just gotten in bed.

"Where the fuck is she at?" Dade asked. He was going ninety miles a minute heading towards SaeKu's room.

"I don't know." Sage was crying on the inside, but kept a frown on her face. "She's not in there."

After Dade double checked SaeKu's bedroom, he went back towards the door. His cell rung, but he ignored it. By the time he made it to the hallway, it was ringing again. Looking down, he saw that it was Lorde trying to reach him. As he picked up, he left Sage with a message. "Come lock up." He ordered. "And tell SaeKu that's her ass when I see her." he slammed the door behind him, causing Sage to fall out laughing.

"You can come out, bitch." Sage yelled. SaeKu had been ducked off in her bedroom bathroom. There was no way she was going to fall into Dade's web, tonight. He had fucked up, and she wanted to stay as far away from him as she possibly could.

**

"Yeah." Dade answered Lorde's call. "Na, dog. Don't say that shit." His chest heaved.

Stopping mid-stride, he held on to the wall for support. It felt as if someone had knocked the win from his lungs. "I'm on my way."

Dade ended the call, and took off running. He needed to make it to the hospital as fast as he could. Lorde had informed him that his mother was coding. She'd been revived more than once, but he refused to have them revive her, again. Lorde was praying she could hold on until Dade's arrival.

Everything was a blur. Dade was unsure how he'd even made it to the hospital, and unharmed. When he made it to the floor that his mother was on, a horrible feeling rushed his bones. He sped up his pace, and made it to her room in record time. As his feet passed her threshold, the sounds of her monitors blaring made him want to turn back around.

Lorde stood at her bedside, void of emotion. He stared, blankly, at her lifeless body, holding back every emotion flowing through his veins. He was too afraid to tap into either, because he knew that he would go ape shit. His mother was his heart, and without her he felt naked. In all of his years, he'd never felt so exposed in his life.

"Sh..." Dade started. He walked closer to the bed, and grabbed Lauren's right hand. Slight movement caused him to peek at the monitor, again.

"Where are the doctors?" Dade asked.

"I told them to let us be. They've been in and out of here for the last hour." Lorde bent down, and unplugged the machines. They were getting on his last nerve with the high pitched sounds that emitted from them. "I knew this was it when I walked in here after they first revived her."

"FUCK!" Dade cussed.

Silence swept the air as the two men watched over their mother's body. No one said a word, even when the doctors came in to remove her tubes and other utensils. Dade was in a state of shock, and Lorde was simply angry at the world.

Once he could contain himself. Dade stepped out of the room –but not before grabbing one of Lorde's phones. He dialed the number that he'd grown familiar with over the past few weeks. His head spun as it began to ring. An angelic wave crossed his path when he heard the voice on the other line.

"Hello." SaeKu crooned.

"She's gone." They were the only words that would surface. Dade's voice cracked at his spoke them. His heart was in unbearable pain, and he desperately needed someone to ease it.

"I'm on my way."

SaeKu ended the call, and jumped out of bed. “Sage.” She yelled.

“What?” Sage yelled back. “Between you and that nigga of yours, I’ll never get any sleep.”

“I need you to drive me to the hospital where Dade is.” SaeKu told her. “I can’t take my car, because I know he’ll need me to drive him back.”

“What happened? Is he okay?”

“Yes. It’s his aunt. I mean, his mother. She just passed.”

“Oh damn. Come on, girl.” Sage threw on her house shoes, and started for the door.

**

“Dade,” she called to him as she made it to the waiting room.

“Yeah.” He lifted his head and answered.

“I’m so sorry.” SaeKu sat beside him, and begin to rub his back. “Where’s Lorde?”

“He just went to the restroom.”

As the words left Dade’s mouth, Lorde appeared from around the corner. His phone was ringing off the hook, but he didn’t bother going into his pocket to answer it. Sage had accompanied SaeKu into the hospital. She saddened when she saw Lorde walk over to the area they were sitting in. Her heart broke for him. He looked like a lost puppy.

Sage wanted to reach out and comfort him, but they didn't know one another like that. She'd seen him fuck a nigga up about putting his hands where they didn't belong. The last thing she wanted to do was tick him off. As Sage observed her surroundings, she realized she was not needed any longer. She thought that she'd better get a move on. Her assignment started in a few hours, and she wanted to be well rested.

"Your phone is blowing up, Lorde. Something may be up." Dade warned.

"Sae, I'm going to get out of here. I need to rest up." Sage stood from her seat.

"Okay. Thanks for the ride." The two hugged.

"No problem, girl. Call me if you need me." Sage headed towards the elevators as she heard Lorde finally answer his cell. As she stepped onto the elevator, she heard footsteps behind her. Looking up, she noticed Lorde getting on as well. He pressed the button for his floor, and watched as the doors closed. It was then that Sage realized she hadn't pressed the "L" for lobby.

As the two rode the elevator in silence, Sage kept stealing glances. Lorde was in the corner with his head hung, low. Feeling compelled to reach out to him, Sage inched closer. As she looked back to see that his floor was approaching, she muscled up the nerve. Stretching her arms out, she wrapped them around his upper body.

Unexpectedly, Lorde embraced her, and begin to weep. His cries were loud and animalistic. Sage was completely blindsided by his actions. Lorde squeezed her, tightly, allowing his emotions to rain from his eyes down onto her pajama top. Sage rubbed his back in a circular motion. She couldn't find the words to say, but her actions were enough.

When the sound of the elevator dinged, Sage's heart broke a little. This was the end of their ride, meaning that they'd both go about their day as if this moment had never happened. It wasn't that she was expecting much afterwards, but she knew that Lorde was hurting and needed to shed the pain he was feeling of loosing his mother. Once that elevator stopped, he would tuck those feelings inside, and that's what she hated the most.

Lorde loosened his grip, and stood up straight. He wiped his eyes and cleared his throat. Stepping off of the elevator, he didn't even bother to give Sage a second glance. Just before the doors closed behind him, Sage reached out her arm to stop them. Peeking out of the elevator, she yelled at Lorde.

"I lost my mother, too." She said.

Lorde turned back at the mention. "And my father." She continued. "Yesterday was their anniversary. One day they were here, and the next day they were gone. I know how you feel." Sage stepped from the elevator.

She reached into Lorde's pocket, and grabbed the iPhone that seemed to be his main line. He didn't have the strength to stop her. Plus, he knew that she didn't mean any harm. "If you ever need anything. Call me."

After handing Lorde his cell back, Sage turned to leave. When she made it to the elevator, she felt her hair begin pulled backwards –in a very sensual way. She attempted to turn her head, but with her hair gripped so awkwardly, the task was impossible.

Lorde's hand rested on Sage's scalp as he brought her body closer to his. He wasn't sure if it was his emotions or hers that was drawing them near, but he wasn't complaining. Leaning down, he pressed his lips against hers. Sage was in utter shock, but went with the flow. The two deepened the kiss after a few seconds, only stopping because they'd both forgotten to breathe within the process.

“I’m sorry about your people. I know that shit had to hurt.”

“It did, but it gets better with time.” Sage sighed. “I need to get going.”

“My daughter is on her way into the world. I’m conflicted. The sense of pride I’m supposed to feel isn’t there. She’s making her entrance on the worst day of my life.”

“Tragic endings makes for beautiful beginnings. That’s your mother, making sure that you’re fulfilled, even in her absence.” Sage pushed the button for the elevator.

Lorde nodded at her parallel. “I never got your name.” he said as she stepped onto the elevator.

“Sage. The name is Sage.” With that, Sage was gone.

On her ride down to the lobby, she reflected over her thoughts and emotions when she discovered her parents had passed. In the midst of her trip down memory lane, Sage began to feel them all over, again. Tears filled her eyes as she walked, swiftly, to her car. The thought of calling in sick crossed her mind. As she’d told SaeKu, she wanted to go spend time with her parents. However, she didn’t want to leave her crew hanging. Figuring she’d visit the minute she got back into town, Sage headed home to get some sleep.

**

Sage’s alarm woke her just four hours after she’d laid down. Her eyes burned from the lack of sleep, and sun shinning in through her window. Her cell rung, nearly scaring her to death.

"Yeah." She answered.

"Are you awake?" SaeKu questioned.

"Yes. I just got up."

"Okay. Just making sure you woke up in time. I'm headed to the airport, now. Can you bring my uniform when you come? We stayed at the hospital the entire time making sure that everything was final. We're just leaving."

"You haven't slept at all?" Sage was feeling SaeKu's pain already.

"Barely. I did catch two hours, though."

"Good. I feel sorry for you, honey."

"Don't. I'll be fine."

"I'll bring your uniform. It's already out, right."

"Yeah." SaeKu nodded as if Sage could see her."

"Alright. See you in a bit."

"Okay."

Sage went to her Pandora station, and played the 90s R&B station. She began to groove as the old school beat chimed in. After hooking her phone up to the loud speaker, she readied herself for a shower. The steam caressed her aches and pains as she tried to get rid of the thoughts about her parents. Lorde's handsome face crossed her mind, causing a smile to tug at the corners of her lips.

Sage had the right mind to touch herself, but she knew that she had to hurry to the airport. A little scoffed that she couldn't self-satisfy, she turned the water off after soaping up and rinsing off. It had been months since she'd been laid, and she'd scratched off each day in her calendar.

The last man she'd dated was a captain, and she wished she'd never set eyes on the tarnished soul.

Stepping out of the shower, Sage dried her goodies and then poured coconut oil over her brown skin. Rocking her waist to the beat, she dressed for work with a smile on her face. After she was completely satisfied with her appearance, Sage rushed into SaeKu's bedroom to get her uniform. She threw the uniform over her arm and snatched the shoes to match. Sage, then, stuffed everything into SaeKu's luggage before pulling it to the door beside hers. Sage ran through, double-checking, the house one last time before her departure.

"Good to go." She gave herself a second thumbs up in the mirror.

Safe opened her apartment door, and was taken back by the surprising presence that awaited her. "Lorde?" she asked with questioning eyes. Peeping out of the door, she checked to see if SaeKu or Dade would be coming around the corner at any minute.

"I got your address from my brother. You going somewhere?" Lorde questioned, admiring Sage in her getup.

"Yeah. Uh." Sage was tongue tied, still unsure of why Lorde felt comfortable enough to show up to her door, unexpectedly. "I have work in a few."

"You trying to make a nigga's life a living hell, right now." Lorde sighed.

"How so?" Sage started pulling, both, her and SaeKu's bags out into the hallway.

"I'm running on e, and needed a place to crash. I just watched my mother take her last breath, and my daughter take her first. It's been a hell of a night, shorty." Lorde confessed. "How much they paying you? I need you to cancel the day or something." He reached into his pocket, and attempted to pull out the wad of money that he was carrying.

"Don't insult me." Sage halted his actions. "As much as I would like to help you, I can't. I have a team that's counting on me to make my next assignment. As well, I can't be bought. When you come to me, come correct. That isn't the way." Sage locked the door to her place, and started down the hallway. Lorde was right behind her, still wondering what to say next. He was perplexed at the notion that she'd rejected his money. If it wasn't money that she desired, he was wondering how the hell he would sway her. Every other female he knew craved the green shit that he liked to spend as much as he made it.

Seeing as though she was struggling with the suitcases, he figured he could start there. Speeding up, he grabbed both of them from her hands and pulled them down the hall. Each of them were quiet until they stepped onto the elevator.

"You need a ride to work?"

"I have a car, Lorde."

"You know what a nigga is proposing." Lorde cut the side eye at Sage, causing her to crack a smile. Her large round eyes lit up at the thought of him not being able to express himself, properly.

"I don't. You're going to have to be a bit more specific."

"I'm parked out front."

"That's only for residents." Sage became alarmed. "They may tow your car."

"I wish a motherfucker would." Lorde chuckled. "I could've parked at the front door, and it's set in stone not to touch the Ashton." Lorde shrugged. "Come on."

"Come on, what?" Sage said as the elevator dinged, and the doors opened. Lorde stepped off of the elevator first, and she was quick to follow.

"Where are you going with my suitcases, Sir? I'm parked this way." Sage questioned.

"You really want to give me a hard time, huh?" Lorde stopped in his tracks, and turned back to Sage.

"Really. I'm not. I just prefer a man who can express himself. Before I just invite myself into your vehicle, I want to be sure that I'm wanted there."

Sighing, Lorde ran his hands down his face. "Sage, let a nigga get you to work."

"That's better, but that poses a problem."

"What's that?"

"If you take me, then how am I going to get back." Sage widened her eyes.

"I guess I'm picking you up, too." Lorde shrugged.

"What if you're busy?"

"Let me know ahead of time, and I'll make sure that I'm free."

"Sounds like a plan."

"So you rolling?" Lorde smiled.

"Yeah. I'm rolling."

Sage followed behind Lorde and admired his attire. He was built so kindly. His jeans sagged, slightly, and his fitted cap hung onto his naked scalp. The three chains that he wore around his neck swung with each step he made. *He looks so nice in blue*. Sage thought to herself. Thoughts of calling in came to mind, but she erased them –quickly. Sage attempted to calm herself as she laid eyes on the beautifully built machine that she'd be driven to work in. A smile crossed her face when Lorde turned back and caught her staring.

"You trying to drive?" Lorde held up his hand, beckoning for her to meet him on the driver side.

"Is that even a question?" Sage replied.

Yeah, this nigga can definitely get it.

"Thanks for coming." Dade grabbed SaeKu's arm and pulled her in for a hug.

"Of course. Of course." SaeKu rubbed Dade's back. "Are you okay?"

Dade had been in a trance the entire time that he'd been seated on the front row of the church. People crowded, the choir song, and friends spoke. However, it was all a blur to Dade. He'd sailed through his aunt's funeral without even being present. Physically, he was there, but his mental hadn't shown up for the gathering.

"The last time we talked, she begged me to forgive my mother." Dade sighed, letting SaeKu go. "Why would she leave on that note? She knows how I feel about that woman and the turmoil that she's caused in my life."

"Listen, she didn't say forgive her today or tomorrow. She knew that it would take time, but she wanted to put the bug in your ear, at least." SaeKu reasoned with him.

"Maybe you're right." Dade appreciated the clarity.

He was thankful that he'd invited SaeKu to the funeral, and Alani had stayed home. Her feet were swollen, and she was suffering from severe back pains. There wasn't any way that she'd survive through the funeral and burial without needing to be taken back home.

"Just give it time." SaeKu rubbed through his curly mane.

Dade grabbed SaeKu's hand, and the two walked towards her car. "You know…" he started. "I could use a ride."

"Well, Sage rode with me." SaeKu turned to find SaeKu. She hadn't run off too far. She searched for Lorde, nearly certain that she'd be near. Just as she thought, she found the two walking in the opposite direction.

"It looks like Sage is good."

"Come on. We can just wait in the car, because I'm not sure if she's going to leave with him."

**

"Here. Let me." Sage insisted.

"Thanks." Lorde placed Pryce in Sage's arms. Her small body was so warm and cozy under the fluffy pink blanket.

"No problem. What were you saying, now?" Sage rocked Pryce's body from side to side. She quieted down almost immediately, surprising Lorde.

"See, why can't she just do that for her pops." He hissed, slick jealous.

"You weren't holding her the correct way." Sage chuckled. "She's a baby, Lorde. You have to be gentle with her."

In the past week, both Lorde and Sage had grown fond of one another. As promised, he'd picked her up from work a few days ago. Since, they'd spoken over three times over the phone, and texted almost every day.

"Na, she just be buggin when she around others. When we're alone, she be cooling it."

"I'd have to see that to believe it. I can't believe her mother would let her out of the house so often. She's only a few days old. She can easily get sick." Sage noted.

"She can?" Lorde had no earthly idea as to what he was doing with a baby, but he was trying.

"Of course. I know you're excited about fatherhood, but baby girl belongs at home with her mother."

"It isn't me." Lorde sighed. "It's her mother."

"What do you mean?" Sage questioned.

"I've been had her since day four."

"She's only seven days old, right?"

"Right."

"Oh God." Sage sympathized with Pryce, immediately. "Well, if you ever need me to get her, then it's fine. I can sit a little here and there."

"I appreciate that shit. For real." Lorde expressed.

"No problem. All I do is sit at home and stare at the walls when I'm not working."

"You trying to get out of the house?" Lorde smirked.

"Should I be?"

"I mean, yeah."

"Are you asking me on a date, Mr. Livingston?"

"Is that what that shit is called?" Lorde chuckled.

"It's nice to see you smile at a time like this." Sage admired his dimples.

"That's the way she would want it."

"I bet."

"Back to this date." Lorde smiled. "You with that shit or what?"

"I don't know. You have to ask me first."

"The fuck you call that shit I just did?"

"I see that this is going to be interesting."

"Can I take you out?" Lorde straightened up, quickly. His black suit made him look more mature and sexy. He was on his grown man shit, and Sage could appreciate that. Her answer was yes, the minute he insinuated a date, but she wanted to make him sweat a little.

"You sure can," Sage nodded.

"Good, because I was coming through anyway… Even if you said no. It's a good thing you didn't though." Lorde shrugged.

"Oh my God." Sage laughed, and followed him towards Dade and SaeKu. They were near her car.

"Aye. I need a favor." He yelled out.

"What's that?"

"I need you to babysit." Lorde didn't sugarcoat shit. He kept it 100.

"The fuck I look like, nigga? You're handing your baby off to the wrong nigga." Dade joked. "I don't even know how to change a damn diaper. She'll return with my draws on."

"Y'all two." SaeKu found the duo amusing.

"I'm taking Sage on a date and shit. I need somebody to keep the kid."

"When y'all trying to go?" SaeKu asked.

"Tomorrow."

"Tomorrow isn't good for me. What about the following day?" she asked.

"That'll work." Lorde nodded. "You down to babysit?"

"Yeah. I'll keep her." SaeKu shrugged.

"Dade, you'd better marry this one." Lorde pointed at SaeKu.

"If she let me, I plan to." Dade rubbed the side of SaeKu's face, causing her to blush.

"I'm about to be out, nigga. You rolling." Dade looked back at SaeKu. He'd planned to ride out with her, but that quickly changed. Sage handed Pryce to her father, and started for the passenger side of the car.

"Yeah. Give me a second."

Lorde walked off, leaving SaeKu and Dade alone. "I'm going to hit you up, so make sure you answer."

"I will. What are your plans for the rest of the day?"

"Keeping up with this nigga, making sure he doesn't off nobody on the strength, today."

"Right. He is one tough cookie."

"That nigga means well, though."

"Well, let me get going."

"Aight. See you later."

"See you later."

SaeKu got into her car after Dade opened the door. He shut it behind her, and blew her a kiss. She turned to Sage, and shuttered. "Girl, that nigga is so fucking fine. Like, how could God have created something so tempting. Was he out to get me or something?"

"Bitch, drive." Sage was cracking up as SaeKu followed directions.

**

"For the twentieth time, you look fine!" SaeKu stuffed another chip in her mouth.

"So, you don't think that I should put on the other shirt?" Sage was a nervous wreck as she prepared for the date with Lorde. She had changed three times, and was contemplating a forth one.

"I told you… NO!" SaeKu yelled.

Before Sage could hit her with a sly comeback, there was a knock at the door. "Thank God!" SaeKu muttered. "About time he's here, because you're driving me up the wall. You've done all of that, and still ended up in outfit number one."

“Kiss ass!” Sage flicked SaeKu off and ran back into her room to put the final touches on her look.

SaeKu took that as her cue to get the door. She opened it to a thugged out Lorde, with a baby strapped on his chest. The sight alone made SaeKu want to burst into laughter, but she held it in.

“Where… How…”

“Don’t even ask.” Lorde shook his head, and walked inside of the apartment. “Help me get out of this shit.”

The pink straps had him all tangled, and he had no clue how to loosen them. “First, let’s get her out of here.” SaeKu laid a blanket on the couch, and grabbed Pryce from the holder. After laying her down, she instructed Lorde to turn around.

“There.” She said as the straps fell from around him.

“Good looking out.” He pulled the baby carrier from his body, and stuffed it in Pryce’s bag. “I put all that baby shit she be needing in there.”

“Ummm…” SaeKu chuckled. “Okay, Lorde.”

“Where Sage at, though?”

“Right here.” Sage stepped from her bedroom, pulling her purse onto her shoulder. She got a good look at Pryce, sleeping away as she greeted Lorde.

“Hey. You ready?”

“I stay ready.”

Rolling her eyes into the top of her head, Sage let out a small giggle before waving SaeKu goodbye. “Where are we going?” Sage thought to ask, after they’d made their way outside. This time, Lorde was pushing his Wagon.

"Hop in." he told her.

"So, where, again?"

"Don't judge me, but I couldn't think of much between now and the last time we talked. I figured we could go to this little hole in the wall that my partner own out east."

"Lorde. Are you kidding me?"

"Na." he started the truck. "I'm dead ass. I even bought you some kicks. I can't have you breaking your leg trying to get out of that bitch. Sometimes them niggas get to dumpin in that hoe."

"Wait. What?"

"Here." Lorde reached into the backseat and produced a box that help a pair of red Giuseppe sneaks. "I hope you can fit them."

"Are you serious right now?"

"I don't know why you always asking me that. Yeah, I'm serious." Lorde placed the box in her lap. "Trust me. You'll thank me later."

"Lorde. Why can't we just go to somewhere that's a little more chill."

"It is chill. I said sometimes that get to dumpin. It don't happen all the time. Besides, do I look like a dinner date type of dude?"

"This is crazy." Sage shook her head, while exchanging shoes.

She was loving the new kick, though. She'd saw them online and made plans to purchase, but hadn't gotten around to it. She wondered how Lorde knew her size, but thought against asking. He might've had some reply about a bitch he used to fuck with looking like she wore the same size. To spare herself the details, Sage just went along with the program.

"Can't knock it until you try it. You might like this little spot."

**

Surprisingly, Sage could agree. She was enjoying herself at the little kickback spot that Lorde had introduced her to. Every nigga in the club had their eye on her, and the same was for Lorde and the hoes. The club and atmosphere had surpassed Sage's expectations, so she made a mental note to visit again.

She made a mental note to keep it relaxed whenever she did return. The women were half-naked, stomach spilling over their too little attire. The guys were more of the same. It seemed like every nigga in the building had the same tee shirt on. Lorde was right about not needing the heels she'd chosen for her fit. Her designer sneakers were perfect for the occasion. While everyone else was looking like they'd spent their last food stamps to get in the club, Lorde and Sage was looking like money.

She had a bottle in front of her as she sat in Lorde's lap. The two were rocking to the beat, as she grinded her hips into his crotch.

"Keep it up, and I'm going to bend that ass over one of these booths."

"Sounds like fun." Sage was under the influence, but well aware of her movements. She was horny as all get out, and the liquor was giving her the courage to act on her emotions.

"Sage, don't play like that." Sex dripped from Lorde's tongue. She was turning him on in the worst way.

"Who said I was playing, Lorde?" Sage rotated her hips, slower.

Reaching around, Lorde cupped her pussy in his hands through her jeans. He was waiting for her to flinch, move his hand, or cuss his ass out. He got neither. Instead, she begin to grind a little harder on him. That was all he needed to see.

"Let's roll." He stood, forcing her to stand, too.

"But the party isn't over, yet."

"Oh, I know." Lorde nodded with promises of a damn good time.

"Where are we going?"

"To the crib. Come on." Lorde grabbed her hand, leaving their bottles for the peasants to drink. He was about to supply someone's buzz for the night, and wasn't complaining.

Lorde walked through the back of the club, in search of his homie Nado. He found him coming from his office, just before he knocked.

"Aye. We out." Lorde told him.

"Aight. Thanks for sliding through. I'm going to have that for you in the morning."

"Take your time, homie. I know it's all there."

"One." Nado raised his hand to salute.

"Come on. It's quicker this way." Lorde took Sage by the hand, again.

They walked briskly from the club to the truck, making it in record time. Both of them made themselves comfortable, as Lorde adjusted his stereo. Sage rested her head on the headrest, and grooved to the sounds of August. Lorde had opted for Pandora rather than his collection of music. As the sounds drowned out his thoughts, he made his way to his crib.

Luckily, Sage was still awake when they pulled in. Her tipsy state lingered as she struggled to get herself from the car. Lorde chuckled at her attempts, and then went around to help her out. She couldn't find the handle all of a sudden.

"Why thank you." She smiled, stepping down.

"You good?" Lorde questioned.

"I'm excellent. You good?"

"Let's go." He grabbed her hand and pulled her towards the house.

Sage didn't have much time to admire that enormous space before her lips were met with soft kisses. After locking the door behind him, Lorde forced her back onto it, sounding with a thud. Sage's smile couldn't be hidden as she licked her lips and watched Lorde remove his tee from over his head.

"You sure you trying to finish what you started?" he quizzed.

"I was thinking you'd never ask."

Sage flung her purse onto the table that was by the door, and started to marvel over Lorde's unclothed frame. She couldn't understand where this ferociousness was coming from, but she was on fire. There wasn't anything that she wanted more in that moment that for Lorde to ride her waves.

Walking up on Sage again, Lorde caressed her backside with his rough hands. He familiarized himself with each curve as he surveyed her body, manually. Her moans heightened his arousal, setting his anticipation of high. Removing himself from her space, he started for the stairs just feet away.

“Come on.” He waved her over.

The two were in high pursuit of his bedroom, touching and feeling on one another the entire way there. Sage was lusting something serious, and hoped that Lorde didn’t take her need for speed the wrong way. She’d been deprived for so long that she lost her entire top at the thought of being laid down.

“Take this shit off.” Lorde insisted when they met the threshold of his bedroom. The midnight blue paradise was a woman’s dream. His personal space was so neatly decorated that Sage was, almost, certain that he hadn’t done it himself.

Being obedient, Sage removed her clothing, one article at a time. While she got undressed, Lorde sat at the edge of his bed, and fired up a blunt that he’d left sitting in his ashtray. The thick clouds of smoke caused Sage’s vision to blur as she searched the darkness for the man of the hour.

After a few tokes, Lorde put the blunt out, and grabbed Sage. He pinned her down on the bed, and blew a cloud of smoke in her mouth. She inhaled, and allowed it to come out of her nose.

“Big shit, huh?”

“I’m not as dual as I appear to be.”

“I see.” Lorde rubbed her fat pussy through her lace thong.

“Ummm.” She moaned, moving her head from side to side.

Lorde was amazed at the amount of moisture that she was able to produce before he even penetrated her. The thought of maneuvering in her oasis prompted his movements. Lorde got on fours, and reached over into his nightstand. He pulled out a condom, and tore the gold wrapper with his teeth. After sliding it onto his erection, he hovered over Sage’s small frame.

Even in the darkness, a dog could find it's way home. Lorde was met with resistance as he tried to enter Sage's palace. After a few tries, he was able to insert himself with ease. Inch by inch, he stretched her pussy to fit his manhood.

"Eeeeewwwwww." Sage moaned from beneath. Lorde was well equipped, and Sage hadn't had much time to prepare herself. His entrance was expected, but the consequences wouldn't be mild. Sage could already sense that her snatch would need a few days to recuperate.

"Damn girl." Lorde called out. Not only was she dripping, but her grip was out of this world. In and out, Lorde stroked her, bringing her satisfaction no matter the direction.

Just as she couldn't, he couldn't keep his groans at bay, either. Pushing Sage's legs above her head, Lorde gave himself complete access to her honey spot. Sage screamed, uncontrollably, as he had his way with her. She was thrown off by his insanely good stroke game. He didn't miss a beat as he rode her to oblivion.

Muscling up the strength, Lorde pulled himself out of Sage, and instructed her to get on all fours. The minute she was in position, he dove inside of her for the second time. She definitely had that snapback, because it was just as hard getting in, again. Lorde shook his head at the thought of how many niggas he was going to body just by looking like they wanted a piece of his pussy.

"I'm cumming…" Sage voiced, convulsing as she began to throw her pussy back on Lorde.

"Shit. Girl." Lorde held on as she rained on his love tool.

The two explored every inch of one another's body as they became well acquainted with what the other liked or appreciated the most. The entire night was filled with sounds of lust and love making. Neither Sage or Lorde gave a damn about it being their first night together when it was all said and done. They were both grown, and both knew that whatever they were started wouldn't end because they decided to take it there on the first night. Sage fell asleep inside of Lorde's arms with a sense of completion.

Chapter Seven

"Come downstairs."

"What?" SaeKu questioned with a smile on her face.

"Come downstairs."

"Dade. I don't have on any clothes, and my hair is a mess." SaeKu smiled through the phone.

"I don't care too much about none of that. Come on down." He ended the call, and waited for her arrival.

"This man." SaeKu smiled.

"This man, what?" Sage rolled her eyes into the roof of her lids.

She was walking through their apartment, rocking and shaking Pryce. It was past her naptime, and she was on fire. The little jitter bug wouldn't go down without a fight. Sage had agreed to keep an eye on her being that it was her off day.

"Is everything."

"It's something about them Livingston men that, us, girls just can't resist." Sage sang.

"Uh. Uh. I don't like the sound of that. What's that supposed to mean? I peeped that you're playing babysitter and shit after one night."

Sage roared with laughter, scaring Pryce and causing her to begin to cry again. "Look what you made me do."

"Na. You're hiding something. I can smell your foul as from afar."

"Whatever. I don't know what you're talking about."

"You fucked him." SaeKu screamed, covering her mouth.

"What?" Sage chuckled.

"Didn't you?" SaeKu asked. "You gave that pussy up on the first night?"

"Dang, you make it sound so bad." Sage frowned.

"Shit, I don't know how you kept it up that long." SaeKu shrugged. "I wanted to jump Dade's bones from the moment I saw him."

"It's really that bad, huh?"

"It is." SaeKu laughed. "I want to hear all the details when I get back. I don't know where this man is taking me, but I'm not turning it down." SaeKu hurried to her room to throw on some clothes.

It was rather warm, so she settled for an oversized tee and a pair of tights. She combed her hair into a messy bun, and brushed down her baby hairs. SaeKu decided on a pair of black converse, and was out of the door. She went downstairs, only to be stunned out of her mind.

Dade was sitting on a yellow motorcycle with his helmet in his left hand, as he leaned over the bikes handle bars –talking on his cell. He resembled something fresh out of a magazine. SaeKu's heart raced as he looked up to acknowledge her presence. His pearly whites glistened as a wide smile stretched his jaws to capacity. Nodding his head, he signaled for her to join him at his side.

The cream distressed tee and acid washed jeans complimented his Nike Huaraches. Dade's line up seemed as if it had been surgically implemented with perfection seeping from it's existence. The sun beamed on his jet black curls that sat on top of his head, leading to the artistic like taper around his sides and the back of his head.

"Are you crazy?" SaeKu exclaimed. "I'm not getting on here to die with you."

"So little faith in your mans." Dade ended the phone call that he was on, and gave SaeKu his undivided attention.

"It's not you. It's these crazy ass New Yorkers. They can't drive a bit."

"That's why I drive for myself and them. Hop on. I have a few stops I need to make."

Huffing, SaeKu placed her hand on her hip, "No speeding Dade."

"What's the fun in riding a motorcycle and abiding by all of the traffic laws?" He stated, sarcastically. "Put this on."

Dade handed her the helmet that was strapped to the back of his bike. He made sure that it was on properly, and secured. "You look good in my shit." He adored her small frame in the large helmet. "Let me get your purse." Dade grabbed the hobo bag and unlocked his seat. He lifted up slightly to place it in the small compartment.

"How clever?" SaeKu commended the creators of his bike.

"Hop on." Dade locked back up, and sat down.

SaeKu threw her right leg over the bike. She seated herself, and then grabbed Dade around the waist. Her nerves were shot, but she was trusting he wouldn't do anything crazy while she was on the bike with him.

"Hold on." Dade yelled, peeling off without warning. SaeKu's face was priceless as he whipped into traffic, weaving in and out of the cars.

As stated, Dade made stop after stop. SaeKu was astonished at the amount of love that the people were showing him. Dade was a hood superstar no doubt. His presence consumed the entire community when he touched down. Children marched from their stoops, dope boys left their corners, and females flocked. It was all routine to Dade, but eye opening for SaeKu.

"That's all you, my nigga." Some kid with a red rag tied around his head asked, admiring SaeKu from behind. His lustful glares made her uncomfortable, causing her to roll her eyes.

"That's all me, nigga. Step the fuck back and focus on your block before I have to unglue your fucking eyeballs from their sockets." Dade hissed. "Fuck y'all find this ole disrespectful ass nigga at?"

"That's Loco, you remember that nigga. He went to the pen for offing his ole man for beating his mamas ass when he was a youngin." J refreshed Dade's memory.

"Aight. Welcome home and shit, Loco, but keep them creepy as binoculars over that way. Ain't shit for you over here." Dade waved Loco off.

"I feel you. When you done, I need to holler at you, though."

"Foco, Loco, whatever the fuck your name is… You're going to have to follow the rules just like everybody else. I don't talk to motherfuckers, not on that note. I have people in place for that shit." Dade was growing more agitated by the second.

"Why you so tight?" Loco questioned. "I just got home, and a nigga trying to keep from going back. Fucking with these nickels and dimes, I'm buying myself a one-way ticket to that bitch." Loco spoke.

"How old are you, kid?"

Dade stopped to pay the kid some attention. He was testing his patience, and Dade could appreciate that. Niggas were timid when he stepped on the scene. Even if they did want a chance, they'd never step to him and ask for one. Loco was fresh out, and risking his well-being for a chance to chase his check.

"I'll be 21 in three months. I ain't trying to be hurting until then."

"You won't be." Reaching into his pocket, Dade handed Loco a burner cell. "As long as you answer when that phone rings."

With that, Dade pulled SaeKu towards the bike, and insisted that she put her helmet on. He did the same, and wished everyone well before cranking his bike and speeding off into traffic. The couple ended up at a small dinner on the left side of the Bronx. It was a little shack that he'd frequented, but hadn't been to in a little second.

"You good?" Dade asked when SaeKu approached their assigned table.

"Yeah. I had to pin my hair back up."

"I see you like the bike, huh?"

"I can't believe I'm saying this, but I do."

"I figured you would. Your life is so fucking monotone. You have to live a little, baby." Dade joked.

"Well, thanks for running my little idea of happiness." SaeKu started to pull out her chair, but Dade swatted at her hands.

"Sit over here." He slid over in the booth that he was seated in.

Once SaeKu was seated, he slid back inside. The waitress came to take their orders, and left them alone again. Dade stirred his water, mixing the lemon that he's squeezed into it. He had a few things on his mind, but wanted to start with the main one.

"I want to make it up to you."

"Excuse me." SaeKu asked.

"The date. I want to make it up to you. I thought about it, and you were right. I shouldn't have run out. That was foolish on my behalf."

"So, now you want to make it up?" SaeKu smirked.

"If you'd let me." Dade nodded.

"You know making up for mistakes never matter as much as the mistake itself, right? I mean… There's nothing a man can do to replace the heartache or heartbreak that he caused a woman in that very moment. Even if his idea of a makeup lifts her off her feet and covers her with happiness and joy… That pain that she felt when shit went left will has already resonated. The makeup is merely the aftermath. Making it up, as you guys love to call it, is like putting icing on a scotched cake. Even though you've spruced it up, the inside is still tarnished."

"MMmmm. Hmmmm." Dade and SaeKu both looked up from one another. They were so lost in their connection that their surroundings played second fiddle. "Hey."

"What's up?" Dade continued to maneuver his straw inside of his water. He could sense the shift in SaeKu's attitude, but tried to remain calm.

"What's up?" Alani laughed, rubbing her swollen belly.

"Yeah. What's up?" Dade repeated himself.

"What's this?" Alani chuckled, nervously.

"What does it look like, Alani? Don't do that. Don't ask shit that you know the answer to." Dade sighed.

"I'm just saying. You went from not knowing this girl to practically eating her face in a public diner." Alani acknowledged SaeKu and Dade's closeness.

Turning back towards SaeKu, Dade said, "My bad about this. You good?"

SaeKu shook her head, and sipped on her sprite. She was better than good. Ticked off a bit, but it had nothing to do with neither Alani or Dade. She was battling a fight within herself.

"Really Dade. I think this is the time to be explaining yourself, but you're worried about if she's okay."

"SaeKu." SaeKu replied. "The name is SaeKu."

"I didn't ask for your fucking name." Alani turned to SaeKu.

"But I told you." SaeKu shrugged. "Address me by my shit, or don't mention me at all."

"I did…"

"Lani, don't even do that. I know you, ma. You're too classy for this shit. Don't embarrass yourself. Hold your head up high and gone about your business. I'll give you a call when I think you've calmed down."

"No! You're leaving, right now. How dare you try to send me off so that you can stay out with her…"

"SaeKu." SaeKu intervened.

"… SaeKu all damn day. If that's what you're thinking, then you've got this all wrong."

"Alani, I'm a grown ass man. I ain't thinking shit. SaeKu is on borrowed time, and seeing as though you're making a huge deal of this shit… I don't have much longer." Dade shrugged. "So, go ahead and get your shit to go. I'll call you later."

"Why?" Alani placed her hand on her hip.

"Because, we need to talk."

"Fuck you, Dade!"

Alani yelled behind her as she stepped away from the table. She knew better than to jump stupid, because Dade had no problem embarrassing that ass for old and new. Alani might've been in her feelings, but she would never cross the line. Dade was the calmest beast she'd ever encountered.

"I just keep fucking up, huh?" Dade sipped his water.

"Cancel our order." SaeKu insisted. "And take me to the crib, yo."

He knew she was pissed, because she never spoke like that. SaeKu was forever gentle with her words. Her tone had changed, dramatically. She tried pushing him out of the booth, but he wouldn't budge.

"We sitting right here, and eating. I'm hungry as fuck and I know that you are, too."

"Move Dade."

"No. You're staying right here. I ain't did shit this time." Dade was honest.

"Did you break it off?" SaeKu asked. "Because you told me a week."

"I have one more day." Dade told her.

"Bullshit."

"SaeKu. I'm serious. I've had too much shit going on to worry about breaking up with Alani. I haven't even seen the damn girl since the day of the funeral." Dade became frustrated.

"Dade, these are all just excuses."

"Excuses? Excuses my ass SaeKu. You're the only damn thing that's been on my mind since you walked your stubborn ass back into my life. I could've been like fuck it and kept pushing, but that ain't how I'm set up. I ain't trying to play you. It's just bad timing for it all." Dade sat back, and turned his attention towards SaeKu. "You think I like this shit? You think I like keeping you in the middle of this shit? Well, I don't this ain't for you, and I know it. However, it doesn't just disappear overnight because we both want it to, either."

"I'm not saying that it will, Dade, but you have to understand my point of view. I feel like we're in some super secret teenage love affair or some shit."

"Super secret? That's what you think this is? Super secret, and I just told the woman I've been in a relationship with for the last nine months to go about her business while we finished up here?" Dade couldn't believe what SaeKu was saying. "I don't see anything secret about that shit. Not once did I downplay this." He pointed between the two of them. "I stayed my ass right here. That should tell you enough."

"Dade, it's not that simple."

"You know what, SaeKu. Fuck this shit." Dade stood. "If you can't see that a nigga is trying his hardest, then you'll never see that. I thought that you'd grown with the years pushing themselves between us, but I was mistaken. All that I'm giving you right now is all that I've got to give. There isn't a woman alive that can say that I've ran behind them for the last what… three or four years… and asked for nothing but a whole fucking bunch of love in return."

"Dade." SaeKu started.

"Na, you're right. This shit ain't working out." He dug into his pocket and pulled out a hundred dollar bill. "Let's go."

"Dade." SaeKu tried to reason with him.

"Let's motherfucking go!" he yelled back, fed up with her need for perfection. She couldn't seem to understand that no love story was perfect, but their hardships would be worth it all in the end.

Without another slip of the lips, Dade made his exit, assuming SaeKu was right behind him. It was five minutes before he noticed she hadn't come out. The blunt that he'd rolled and fired up while standing outside was still lit when he walked back inside of the restaurant to find her still seated –eating the food that she'd ordered.

"What are you doing?" Dade frowned.

"I'm eating. What does it look like?"

"I don't have time for this bipolar ass shit."

"I'm not asking you to stay. I called a ride. I'm good."

"Who did you call?" Dade's antennas went up.

"A ride." SaeKu replied.

"Who? Don't fucking play with me, SaeKu."

"Gone about your business, Dade. I'll be good."

Pulling on the blunt that was in his hands, Dade shook his head. "I don't know what the hell a nigga going to do with you." He inhaled and, then, blew out smoke.

"Nothing. I figured it's time to just be honest with ourselves, and go our separate ways."

"That's not an option." The sound of being without SaeKu was all fucked up. Dade wasn't having that shit. "I'm going to fix this. If it's the last thing I do, I'm going to make sure that you understand how deep this shit with us runs. I love you, girl." Dade leaned forward, and grabbed SaeKu's jaws. He bent and placed a kiss on her lips. "I'm going to fix this. Just give me a little time."

With that, he was back out of the door. Before his foot could meet the pavement, SaeKu had placed his cell back on the block list. She didn't have time for the back and forward. Her heart was not some toy, and she refused to be played with. The next time Dade stepped to her, he'd better be coming correctly.

**

"Where's Sage?" Lorde asked when SaeKu opened the door.

"How do y'all niggas keep getting past security?" SaeKu blew out in frustration.

"Does it actually look like security wants to put his dick beaters on me?" Lorde lifted his black tee, and exposed the two glocks sitting at his waist sides. "Exactly. Now, where that girl at?"

"She's finishing up her makeup." SaeKu stood aside, and allowed Lorde to walk in.

"Na, she might as well come on. We fucking, tonight. She ain't going to even need all that on her face… fucking up my sheets and shit." Lorde stomped through their apartment.

"You're early," Sage turned to face Lorde when he walked into her bedroom. She was trying to play it off, because she was the one running behind.

"Run that on somebody else. Don't even worry about putting no more of that on your face. We about to be out. All of that shit is going to be smeared by the end of the night, anyway, so ain't no sense in caking it up." Lorde started picking up her makeup pallets, placing them in her makeup bag. "Come on."

"Boy move. I have one more lash to put on, and I'm done."

"Nawl. You good like that. Come on." Lorde insisted.

"Lorde, move. I'm not having sex with you, tonight. The other night was a slip up, so don't get the big head." Sage rolled her eyes.

"So, at what point did you notice… Before or after you slid that pussy up and down this dick?" he asked, foul like. "Girl, bye. Get up, and let's go."

"Where the hell did you put my other lash?" Sage ignored Lorde, and begin looking for her lash.

"I threw it in the bag. Let's go."

"I'm not going anywhere with one lash on."

Looking Sage up and down, Lorde saw that she was fully dressed. A smirk crossed his lips as he thought of his next move. "You'd better not!" Sage called his bluff, but he fooled her.

Scooping her up from the ground, he threw her over his shoulder, grabbed her purse, and darted from her room.

Sage was in tears as he ran through the apartment with her head bouncing up and down.

"How's Dade?" SaeKu mustered up the nuts to ask. It had been three days since she'd blocked him, and she was missing him like crazy.

"Call that nigga and see." Lorde didn't bother to look back. He and Sage were out of the door in a flash.

"I can't stand you!" Sage slapped Lorde across the back. She pulled off her one lash as they stepped foot on the tracks. They'd opted out of a nice time at a fine diner, and chosen to hit the race tracks to watch a few races instead.

"Whatever, you don't need all of that shit on, anyway." Lorde waved her off.

"What's up?"

"What's good?"

"You aight?"

Lorde was being greeted from every angle, but his nods and waves were very few.

"Why aren't you speaking back to these people?" Sage laughed.

"I only have words for the trill niggas. The rest of these motherfuckers are pussy." Lorde shrugged, pulling Sage into his grasp. As they neared the bleachers, he spotted a familiar face – one that he could never forget. It was the face of the trifling ass bitch that he'd chosen for a baby mama.

"Type of shit I be talking about. If this bitch is here, then where the fuck is my daughter." Lorde hissed, pulling Sage's hand along with him. Her eyes narrowed to slits as she zoomed in on Lorde's prey. Her stomach knotted at the thought of how left shit was about to go.

"While you out here auctioning your leaking ass pussy off, where the fuck is my daughter?" Lorde questioned.

"She's good, nigga. It ain't like you give a fuck, anyway. You're out here with this bitch instead of at home with her." Gia turned to face Lorde, ready for a showdown. However, her problem was with Sage rather than her baby daddy.

"Lorde…" Sage called, not feeling the way that she was being disrespected.

"This bitch has seeing about your kid more than you have since you pushed her out of that fucking trap house you call a vagina, so have some fucking decency when you're speaking to the stepmother of your kid." Lorde pointed out, shocking both Gia and Sage.

"In your fucking dreams, Lorde."

"Where is she, Gia?" Lorde questioned, gritting his teeth.

"She's at the crib?"

"With who?"

"My people. Who the fuck else?"

"Your people, bitch you're saying that like that's supposed to make a nigga feel any better. They're worse off than you, and one would think it doesn't even get any worse."

"Like I said, she's with my people."

"Bet. Gia. I swear… You'd better beat me there, because if a hair on my daughter's head is out of place then that's your ass." Lorde didn't give her a chance to answer before he stormed off. Gia knew not to be on no dumb shit, so she took off behind him. Sage was confused, but she was trailing behind him as well. He still had a grip on her hand, so she had no other choice but to keep up.

He wanted to do his baby mama dirty in front of the entire crowd that had come to the show, but he refrained. What they didn't know was that Gia's entire family was sprung out on dope. Lorde was surprised that she'd slipped through the cracks. It was that damn bad. Her people were fucked up in the head. They couldn't even care for themselves, less known a kid. Pryce belonged with her mother, and Gia knew it. However, she was too selfish to even give a fuck. It was baffling as to how a woman could carry a child for over nine months, and want absolutely nothing to do with it after it was born. Gia was a pathetic ass bitch, and Lorde was going to show her better than he could tell her that night.

Lorde did the dash getting to Gia's crib. When he made it there, he hopped out, barely putting his truck in park. He beat the door down like he was the cops, search warrant in hand. An older man opened the door, and the two exchanged words before Lorde went inside of the house, and then came back out. He was carrying Pryce's car seat when he appeared, again. Before he could make it to the truck, headlights could be seen turning into the driveway.

Gia's loud mouth could be heard from afar. "Put my baby down, Lorde. Gone about your fucking business." She yelled, finger in the air.

"Get the fuck back while I've got my daughter in my hand." He warned. "I'm two seconds off of your ass for this foul ass shit you pulled, so back up."

"Na. You aren't taking her anywhere."

"If you know what's best for you, you'd back up, my G." Lorde's voice cracked.

Sage could hear his distress call, and opened her door to come to his rescue. Of course she didn't want to get in the middle of their drama, but a child was involved. If Lorde said that they were taking Pryce, then they were taking her with them. There was no questioning the fact. The underlying pain behind Lorde's words let Sage know that something just wasn't right.

"Give me my fucking daughter." Gia reached at the carseat. Lorde sat that seat down, and hiked up his pants. The next sound you heard was Gia gasping for air. Lorde had grabbed her by the neck, and slammed her body to the ground.

"Lorde!" Sage yelled.

"Stay the fuck out of this." He warned. "Bitch, I want to end your shit right fucking now, but for the sake of my daughter I'm letting you live." Lorde wanted to sock soul to Gia, but he settled for mushing her in the face with an open hand.

His frsutratoins were at an all time high as he looked at the piece of filth that he'd once wifed up. "You're a fucking disgrace. You won't see Pryce again until I feel like it. You don't deserve her!" Lorde smashed his finger into Gia's face, over and over.

"Lorde. Please." Sage called out, picking up Pryce's car seat.

Lorde listened to Sage's pleas, and stood from the ground. He was piping hot as he saw Gia lift up right after him. He wanted to break every bone in her body, but decided to spare Sage the torture. He walked off, and attempted to help Sage get Pryce's car seat strapped into his truck. Before he knew it, Sage was yelling, attempting to get his attention. He turned to see Gia coming at him with a brick in her hand.

Lorde instantly ran towards her, full force. Realizing her mistake before she could even make it, Gia dropped the brick, and took off running for the house. She didn't get too far before her 26-inch Indian weave was wrapped around Lorde's fingers. He pulled her all the way to the ground before pulling his pistol from his waist, and placing it in her mouth.

Pulling the trigger, he imagined sending one to her dome, but he only heard a click. Gia's skimpy shorts were soaking wet, convinced that she'd be floating down to hell any minute now. "I've killed niggas for stepping on my shoes on a good day." Lorde gritted.

He was well aware of what pistol he'd pulled from his waist. One was loaded, without it's safety feature on. The other was loaded, without one in the chamber –plus it was on safety.

"I'm sorry." Gia finally found her voice.

"Gia, if you know what's best for me… I suggest you stay away from my daughter."

The car ride was silent, as Sage fumed. She thought that Lorde's behavior was unacceptable. After tonight, she wanted nothing to do with him. If this was how he treated his women, then he could go about his life as if they'd never met. She didn't care for the ghetto brawls or constant disrespect. Her life had been peachy without any drama, and she wanted to keep it that way. The dick was good, but not good enough to throw away her common sense.

"I've never put my hands on a woman before." Lorde had to get shit clear, because he could just imagine what Sage was thinking. "She left my daughter with a crack head child molester." He informed her.

Turn this bitch around, you ain't beat that hoe good enough. Sage thought, but was careful not to voice her opinion. Gia was on some other shit, and she wanted to square up with her. There wasn't any way that she was supposed to leave her child with a crack head who molested children.

Sage was silent for once.

"The same nigga she left Pryce with used to fuck with her when she was a kid."

Sage was still in shock. Instead of talking, she just listened.

"Say something." Lorde demanded.

"I can't do this, Lorde." That was all that she had to say.

"Do what, Sage? I ain't asking you to do nothing but show a nigga some love and affection."

"At what price, huh?" Sage turned to face him. "This is only date two, and you're pulling guns and beating bitches. What will date four look like? Huh? A fucking drug war? Come on. Tell me."

"Don't go there. I would never put you in the middle of no shit like that."

"You just did!"

"That was different. I knew in my heart that my baby wasn't safe. I did what any other man would've done for their child. If you can't understand that shit, then I don't know what to tell you."

"Right. That's exactly what I'm saying. This shit is pointless." She pointed between them. "Because quite frankly, I don't understand the half of it."

Sage tuned Lorde out as he continued to plead his case. She wasn't worried about a thing he was saying. She'd made it up in her mind that she was done with whatever the hell he was trying to cook up. If, ever, he needed assistance with his baby girl, then she'd try to help him out. However, their ship had sailed.

When Lorde pulled up to Sage's complex, she grabbed her belongings, and hopped out of the car. She, then, went around back and opened the door. Lorde was stunned when she unstrapped Pryce's car seat, and grabbed her diaper bag that he left inside of his whip for emergencies.

"What are you doing?" Lorde questioned.

"I have the next few days off. Come get her by Sunday. You need some time to cool off. Plus, you don't even have a sitter, yet. You need to work on hiring a nanny." Sage informed him.

"I'll get on that ASAP. You don't know any?"

"I'll see what I can find out."

"Good looking out. I'll hit you up in the morning."

"Don't."

"What you mean, don't?"

"Just what I said, Lorde. This shit is not me, aight. I'm not taking it there with you. I have morals and boundaries, and you're pushing up against them all."

"You ain't giving me a chance. You just out without even looking at this shit from my angle."

"Lorde. Like I said… Come get Pryce by Sunday."

"I'm calling your big forehead ass in the morning, so pick up the fucking phone."

"Save yourself the hassle."

"Sage."

"Goodnight Lorde."

With that, Sage slammed the truck door. Once inside of her apartment, she rushed to get Pryce a fresh bottle. She'd gotten a bit cranky on the way up. After fixing a small bottle, she pulled Pryce out of her car seat, and marveled over her beautiful brown skin. Her eyes were a light shade of brown, and she had curly locs all over her head. Strangely, her cheeks were blush colored, and her hair was nearly orange in color. Pryce was a doll, and Sage loved having her around. She'd grown on her, and like a proud mother, she felt a sense of ownership over the precious little being.

"Hey baby girl. You going to spend some time with SaeKu and I. We're going to have a girls weekend. Sounds fun, right?" Sage spit out baby talk until Pryce's bottle was empty, and her lids were heavy. The two made it to Sage's bed just in time for them both to call it a night. Sage fell asleep with Pryce in her arms, and wouldn't have rather had it any other way.

Chapter Eight

"Girl, tell me about it. Them and these damn babies are going to run us both into the ground." Sage chuckled, getting Pryce's belongings together. "I'm not even trying to go that route, though."

"Me either. Like, seriously."

"Girl, boo. I have a feeling that Dade is not going anywhere any time soon."

"So you have no faith in me, huh?" SaeKu grabbed her chest as if she was appalled.

"I don't. Sorry, boo!"

"It's cool, though. I have no faith in you either. You've got that nigga on block, yet his precious baby girl has been with you since you put his ass on block." SaeKu called Sage's bluff. She had yet to understand how she could be so upset with a man, but still care for his child. One would think that Sage had birthed Pryce as much as she had her.

"Leave her out of this." Sage burst into laughter. "He should be out there, now."

"Knowing him, he's been down there arguing with security for the last little bit."

"Exactly, but if they let him up… I swear to God!"

Sage and SaeKu had both went to complain about the security allowing unwanted guest up. They'd been sure to clarify that they wanted neither Dade or Lorde having access to their floor. Their complaints had been taken into consideration, because neither Lorde or Dade had come knocking –even though they both had every reason to.

"They're not going to let that maniac up here."

"Good, because… I don't even have words for that scenario."

"Is she good to go?"

"Yes. She's all good." Sage saddened. "I hate that my pookie has to leave me." Sage leaned down and planted kisses all over Pryce's face. Her world lit up as Pryce stared back at her, kicking her feet and hands.

"Let the girl breathe, Sage."

"Girl, bye." Sage continued to shower Pryce with love. "I'm going to miss her."

"You'll be right back, and she'll be right back over. She may even bring a friend next time –one by the name of Lorde."

"Fuck you!" Sage lifted up and flicked SaeKu off. "Here." She handed her the bag.

When SaeKu reached the lobby of their apartments, Lorde was near a brawl with the staff. She shook her head, and called out his name. He was stunned to see that it was her instead of Sage. He'd been communicating with Sage about picking up Pryce from one of his burners. He was hopeful that he's see her, being that she seemed cool over text. SaeKu's presence said otherwise.

"She really on this shit?" Lorde questioned.

"Hey, Lorde." SaeKu ignored his question. "Everything is in her bag. We went out and got her a few new outfits to hold her over until the next time she visits, which Sage wants to be in four days by the way." SaeKu threw that out.

"So, she couldn't come down and tell me that shit? And what's with this shit about me being band from going upstairs." Smoke was coming from his ears as he recited words.

"I don't know." SaeKu shrugged. "That's something you'll have to ask her."

"She really tripping. That's cool. I've got something for that ass."

"See you later Pryce." SaeKu handed Lorde the car seat before leaning down and pecking her sweet cheeks.

SaeKu headed back upstairs to get on Sage's nerves. "That man is going to rip you a new asshole. I don't know why you're playing."

"I'm not. I'm done with his ass. That shit was just too much for me. I can do without the dramatics." Sage swore up and down she was done with Lorde, but something within kept telling her that she wasn't. Either way, she was riding her current decision until the wheels fell off.

"Don't say I didn't warn you!" SaeKu laughed,

**

SaeKu made it to the airport just in time to make her assigned flight. Since she'd handed Pryce over to her father, she'd been on a mission. She needed new identification, being that she'd left her purse under Dade's seat the day they had their blow up. She refused to call and ask for it, so she went and got new identification instead.

"I thought you wouldn't make it in time." Sage handed her a cup of caramel coffee from Starbucks. They rarely got to fly together, so this was a celebratory moment.

"I thought I wouldn't either. God is good, though, girl." SaeKu high-fived Sage. The two stepped onto their flight, and begin to check the cabins before the passengers begin to board.

"You ready?" Sage called out, ironing the wrinkles that were in her skirt out.

"Yes." SaeKu smiled after glossing her lips for a final time.

35,000 feet in the air, SaeKu sat in the back of the plane, going through her image gallery. Dade's photos were few and far apart, but she appreciated the sight of each of them. Her heart rang each time she swapped, hoping that his face would be the next to pop up.

"Thirty minutes before landing." Sage called out to her, causing her to look up from her phone.

"Okay." SaeKu shoved her phone into her robe before standing up –getting her feelings in check. She wanted, so badly, to reach out to Dade, but she knew that it wasn't the best decision on her part.

The two walked down the aisle, being sure that everyone had their trays and seats upward with their seatbelts on to prepare for landing. It was another two hours before SaeKu was inside of her hotel, fresh out of the shower, and preparing for her second flight. It wouldn't be pulling out for another four hours, but she wanted to get a quick nap in. Otherwise, she would have stayed at the airport and waited it out.

A knock on the door stirred her from her just shy of an hour since she'd laid her head down to rest. "Sage. Go away." She yelled at the door.

SaeKu realized Sage wasn't going anywhere after the second set of knocks. Sighing, she lifted from the bed and headed to the door. Pulling her robe together, she opened the door, and got the surprise of a lifetime.

Dade Livingston stood before her with stress written over his handsome face. His eyes were low, airing out his secrets. He'd been chiefing before he had come into her presence. He was dressed in a pair of black sweats, black tee, and a single chain hung fro his neck. He brushed his hand through his goatee, with his head cocked to the side, making SaeKu cream all over the inside of her thighs.

"You forgot this." He lifted her purse.

Appalled and turned on to the fullest, SaeKu was at a lost for words.

"I miss you, SaeKu." Dade admitted, leaning against the frame of the door. "I didn't come to fight or ruin your night. I just needed you to know that… and give you this." He handed her the bag that she'd left on his bike.

"You flew out here just to give me your purse?"

"And to see your face. I've tried back home, but you told the people on a nigga. This was the only way."

"How did you know where I was?"

"Sage."

"I'm going to get her."

"Don't worry, though. She doesn't know that Lorde is here. I think that's punishment enough."

"You're right." SaeKu sighed. "Thanks, Dade."

SaeKu tried closing the door, but Dade blocked it. "You miss me?" he had to know. The question had plagued his mind since the day that they'd gotten into their spat.

"Dade. Thanks." SaeKu avoided his question, intentionally.

"I'm a single man, now, SaeKu." He smiled.

"Have a nice night, Dade."

"I sure will, Ms. Noble." Dade stood up straight. "I'll see you around."

SaeKu closed the door of her hotel room, and ran to the bed. She climbed on top, and jumped up and down like a kid. Her wish had finally come true, and her lover was a free agent. His visit assured her that hope was dead, and they still had time to get their thing right.

Blopping down, she allowed herself to catch her breath before opening her purse. Out of curiosity, she wanted to know if all of it's contents were still in place. As expected, they were. However, there was an addition to the contents she'd left inside. Pulling out the folded sheet of paper, SaeKu read the words that had been scribbled. After a few seconds, she held the note to her chest, and began to weep. Her happy ending was just beginning.

Can we start, again? Yes or No?

The simple words were music to SaeKu's ears. She had to contained her excitement, promising not to give Dade a reply until the morning. He deserved to wait a while.

"Boy! Are you crazy or what?" Sage was upset with herself for opening the door without double checking to be sure that it was SaeKu. Now, she was pinned up on the wall while Lorde had his way with her. Of course she appreciated the gesture, but he was making it hard to keep her word. She wanted to be done with him, and here he was. She kicked her own ass for even spilling the beans to Dade. Her plan had backfired, tragically.

"Why you been dodging me?" Lorde asked as he made his way down Sage's body.

Here eyes bulged out of their sockets at the thought of him pleasing her orally. She thought that she'd have to force the task on him rather than him willingly participating.

"Lorde. Stop." Sage insisted, but not really.

"We miss you, Sage." Lorde rubbed her soft spot, and then nibbled at it through her underwear. "You don't miss us?" he asked, referring to his dick.

"Lorde." Sage's head fell backwards, and her legs spread a bit more. She was near an orgasm, and the young man had barely touched her.

"Tell me you miss us." He reached up and moved her panties over. Using his tongue, he stretched it along the length of her pussy. "Say it."

"Uhhhh." Sage cried out.

"Say it." He slid one finger inside of her as he continued to lick on her vagina.

"I missed y'all." She caved, and that was about all that Lorde needed to hear. His dick was screaming to be freed. However, he was patient. He didn't lift himself from the floor until her cream was flowing down her face.

Their lips met as he unleashed the beast between his thighs. Lorde, then, spun Sage around, and forced her to bend over. Her hands planted themselves on the wall, as she waited, impatiently, for Lorde to enter her. She ignored the fact that they didn't have protection, and went with the flow.

"AHHHHH." She cried out when he finally found her opening.

Lorde pushed himself in, and nearly lost his fucking common, book, and street sense in one stroke. Sage's pussy was to die for, literally. He'd put the pistol to any nigga head that dared to get near it, and blast his fucking brains.

"Girl, if you ever give this shit up… I'm going down for double murder. I'm killing you and that fuck nigga." Lorde wasn't the most romantic guy, but he was always honest. He said what he felt, at any giving moment. Sage wanted to end their session at the sound of murder, but threw all caution to the wind. The dick was already feeling too good for her to rationalize.

Back and forth, Lorde long stroked her tunnel with his thick chocolate pipe. When it was all said and done, Sage's back was planted on the hotel floor as they both attempted to catch their breath.

"Where's Pryce?" Sage asked.

"I let my mother's best friend keep her for the day."

Sage didn't say much else, because she was already wishing she hadn't have given into Lorde. Now, he was going to think everything was back on track, but it wasn't. She wanted to mention it, but decided against it. Sage was on a high, and not quite ready to come down.

"Can I tell you something?" Lorde asked.

"Yeah." Sage laid beside him.

"I'm sorry that you had to see that the other night. I would never put my hands on you." He confessed. "You don't understand what that shit did to me. She left Pryce with a man that played up her ass as a youngin." Lorde tried to get Sage to understand where he was coming from.

"Why don't you just ask her to sign over her rights, Lorde. It's obvious that she wants nothing to do with Pryce. I figure it's only right."

"I don't want to take Pryce away from her mother."

"Just because you push a baby out of your pussy, that doesn't make you a mother. You're the closest thing to a parent that little girl has."

"And you…"

"I'm just helping out, Lorde."

"I appreciate it, though." He admitted. "That's why I'm trying to get you back in my life. I need someone like you on our team."

"Lorde."

"Don't think about it, now. Give it some time, and get at me."

Lorde stood from the floor, and walked into the bathroom. Sage remained on the floor as she listened to him clean himself up and get ready to leave. "Here." He pulled stack after stack from the backpack that Sage hadn't even noticed until now. "Dade said y'all flying to a couple of cities, and won't be back until a few days. I figured you could have yourself a good time while you were there –on me."

"You don't have to do that."

"But I want to. It's not bribery money or no shit like that." Lorde chuckled. "If you don't spend it, fuck it. Putting in your savings or something. I don't care. It's yours, though."

"Thanks."

"I'm out. Stay up. One."

Lorde left the room without another word. His cologne lingered in the distance, causing Sage to miss him already. It was something so profound about his presence that made her crave him. However, she knew damn well she didn't need him.

Damn you, Lorde. She thought as she pulled herself from the floor.

**

SaeKu took Dade up on his offer to begin, again. A few days after she landed, they'd planned a romantic date. They'd both laid their cards on the table, and aired out their concerns. With a bit of trust, they both felt as if they would be able to surpass all that had been placed in their path –in the pursue of their destruction.

SaeKu was filled with content at the thought of their plates being clean, and being able to explore one another as their chosen partners. The entire night, her ears and cheeks were on fire. She'd smiled more in one night than she had in years. For once, she felt whole, and it had everything to do with Dade. As promised, he'd fixed all that he'd broken.

After their date, SaeKu allowed Dade to talk her into going home with him, after assuring her that he wouldn't try anything funny. SaeKu wanted to omit sex from their regimen for the first sixty days of their reunion. She wanted them to connect on levels other than sexual, and he understood her –fully.

The entire ride to his home, he stole quick glances at her. In the dark, it was hard to see much of her melanin coated skin, but just her silhouette was enough. She seemed genuinely happy, being that the smile she wore hadn't disappeared all night. Dade took note at the fact that shit felt better that way. He wanted to be the one putting the smile on her face rather than taking it away.

Dade was relieved that the gap between he and SaeKu had been bridged. Finally, the two were able to place aside the differences that they shared in order to make their thing work. Pushing his key into the keyhole, he turned to a beaming SaeKu. As he mentally double checked his proceedings, being sure that he'd cleared all traces of Alani, he twisted the key and knob – simultaneously.

"I enjoyed you, tonight." He pulled SaeKu into the house behind him, wrapping his arms around her waist, and inhaling her scent. "Welcome home."

"Welcome home, huh?" SaeKu chuckled. "Is that right?"

"It is." Dade nodded, pulling her through the foyer.

SaeKu's eyes traveled through the house faster than her feet. Every fixture, article, picture, furniture piece, vase, mirror, and light she fell head over heels in love with. Properties on the outskirts were the best to settle in, and Dade had snagged a luxurious piece of the pie. SaeKu could only dream of having a place as large and lavish as his. After a grand tour of Dade's home, SaeKu reminded Dade of the promise he'd made at dinner.

"This is my home as much as it is yours. You may as well get acquainted baby girl. You'll be spending more time here then I will be." Dade tapped SaeKu's ass, and then headed towards the shower.

"I doubt that."

"We'll see. Grab you some boxers and a tee shirt or some shit. I'd prefer you went to bed without either, but I'll play fair since we're trying this dating thing out and shit. A promise is a promise."

"Exactly." SaeKu nodded. "Thanks Sir."

"My pleasure Madam. Don't get too happy, though. I don't know how long I can keep this shit up. I prefer my dick wet, and I don't mean from no fucking water either." Dade winked, and left SaeKu inside of his bedroom. "If you change your mind, then come join me in the shower." He yelled back.

"I'll just get in with you, but don't touch me." SaeKu replied, busying herself with finding something to throw on once she emerged from the shower.

On the first shot, SaeKu was able to find a pair of boxer briefs that looked as if they would fit. The challenge ensured when she attempted at finding a tee shirt that didn't swallow her whole. Draw after draw, she pulled opened, only to find more boxers.

"Gosh, this man has more underwear than me." SaeKu giggled –pulling another drawer open.

Her stomach curled in knots, and her pretty little head began to spin as she stared at the contents of the fourth drawer she'd opened since her search started. A pain surged through her chest, reflect'ng the pain that had started at her dome, and was working its way through her being.

Confusion set in, and anger was sure to follow. The doubt that she'd swallowed at the top of her night had resurfaced, proving her intuition to be insightful. Squeezing her eyes together, SaeKu wished away the sight before her. When she opened her eyes, she prayed that it would be replaced with a more suitable one.

Dade cleansed his body as waited for SaeKu's arrival. She'd taken longer then expected to join him, so he'd begin without her. An unsettling feeling caused a rumble in his abdomen area. Something wasn't right.

Leaving the shower running, Dade stepped out, and grabbed a towel to wrap around his body. Hesitantly, he walked into his bedroom, and his worst nightmare had become his reality. Dade seemed to never be able to catch a break when it came to the woman he loved. Once the good guy, as of lately he seemed to have flipped the switch. It was the furthest from the truth, and he was hopeful of the fact that SaeKu realized it.

Clenching his jaws, he chastised himself for not Alani proofing his home before inviting SaeKu over. He was, nearly, certain that he'd removed everything that was connected to her out. However, he'd sadly been mistaking. SaeKu stood directly in the same spot that Alani had stood each morning as she pulled out skimpy pieces of underwear to cover her light skin.

With Dade's presence noted, SaeKu lifted her head from the position that it had been subjected to for the last umpteen seconds. Turning to face her heart's assassin, she nodded her head and pushed the drawer to the dresser closed as best she could.

SaeKu's mind went into overdrive as she searched for her shoes with her eyes. Her head pounded at the thought of putting the uncomfortable heels on, so she opted out of the task.

Lifting her skirt, she struck out for the door. SaeKu had no clue where she'd go or how she'd get there, but being in Dade's presence was not an option.

Like the beautiful Cinderella, leaving behind her glass slipper, SaeKu tucked her skirt under her fingertips, and fled. As she ran through the lavish dwelling, her pedicured toes contacted with the marble floors while the tail end of her skirt brushed its surface.

"SaeKu!" she heard from behind her.

Too afraid to turn around, SaeKu continued ahead of her. Dade's footsteps could be heard in the distance, nearing her by the second. Reaching out, SaeKu unlocked the restraints that held her captive behind the castle style front door that she loved so much. SaeKu swung the door open, not bothering to close it behind her. Her feet tapped the concrete of Dade's porch, alerting her that she'd reached freedom.

"SaeKu!" Dade yelled, "FUCK!"

Dade stumbled over his own two feet as he tried catching up to SaeKu. She was fast on his feet, but he was quicker. Picking up speed, he chased her down, catching hold onto her top, barely. "Slow down." He sighed, snatching her back.

The two neared his Rolls as he flung SaeKu onto the hood of it. "Why do you keep running?" he questioned, but SaeKu would not answer. His breathing was labored, and his heart rate had sped up, tremendously.

The thought of her slipping from his grasp because of a crucial mistake on his part had him scared out of his mind. He wouldn't have known what to do if he'd finished his shower to find her long gone. It had been long enough for the two of them. Anymore time apart would be agonizing.

SaeKu's head was turned in the opposite direction, afraid that she'd resent the sight of his handsome face if her eyes landed on him.

"Huh?" Dade gritted. "Why do you keep running, SaeKu? Explain that shit to me."

"Because you keep fucking up!" SaeKu yelled back, still not giving him the satisfaction of looking into her doughy eyes.

"Look at me." He grabbed the bottom of her face, and forced her to stare back at him. "I love your ass, aight. There isn't a single soul in this world that I want more than I want you, but you've got to put on your big girl draws and toughen up. You can't be running at the sign of trouble when fucking with a nigga like me."

"This isn't what I want. In fact, this shouldn't be what anyone wants."

"What you want, SaeKu? Just tell me, because you aren't leaving. If you want to yell, cuss my ass out, or tell me to go fuck myself, then have your way. But tonight, you can hang that shit up. You're running from a disaster that YOU created from running in the first place. So, what is it? What you trying to do?"

WHAP!

SaeKu sighed as she slapped Dade's beautiful blemish-free skin due to the aggression that she was feeling. That's what she wanted. She wanted him to feel the same sting that she was feeling, even if it wasn't in his chest. He was left in utter shock, but it wore off within a millisecond. Nodding his head, he understood her frustrations.

"I'm going to give you that one. I know you're upset, ma, but that ain't even you. Don't ever do that shit, again. Don't ever let someone else's actions depict your character or cause you to act in a way that you normally wouldn't. That's for suckers, not you, me. Now… Let me fix this shit. Come inside. You've got me out here in a fucking towel and shit." Dade said, looking down at the white towel that clung to his lower half.

"Do you love her?" SaeKu questioned, afraid of the response that she'd received. It was a true statement that women asked questions that they knew they didn't want the answer to. Right after the words left her mouth, SaeKu regretted them.

Dade's movements were delayed as he kept his head down. "You worried about the wrong…"

"Well, do you?" SaeKu's voice softened as she awaited his reply.

"I have only loved two women in my life time. Lauren Livingston and SaeKu Noble." Dade admitted, and was truthful in every sense of the word.

"Then why is…"

"She stayed here a lot, aight. She just moved her shit in. I didn't approve it, but I didn't speak on it, either. That shit is dead, though. I broke it off, SaeKu. It's you, ma. It's all you. You keep running, and I keep chasing you. This time, I'm not letting you get away from a nigga, so you may as well pull back those layers that are keeping you guarded and let me in, girl." Dade reached upward and grabbed SaeKu's neck.

"This isn't how I imagined it." SaeKu blew out a gush of air. "Some things that you're asking me to overlook, I can't… Like this."

"Fuck it. Come on. I forgot to clean out the draw, but we're about to clean the motherfucker off together." Dade pulled SaeKu in his direction.

She, stubbornly, allowed him to guide her back into the house. She was tired of the back and forth, but her heart and her mind weren't in sync. While one said run, the other said stay. She was at a tug of war, and wanted it to end –desperately.

"Where were you planning to run to without any shoes on?" Dade asked, sliding her the house slippers that he had by his door. "Put these on before you get sick."

"I was going wherever my feet would take me."

"Man, you ought to be tired of that shit. You can only run for so long, SaeKu. It's time out for that."

SaeKu remained quiet, understanding where he was coming from, but understanding her deposition as well. They reentered the bedroom, together. Dade went inside of a small closet in the corner, and produced a new sheet set, and a recycled bag.

"I've changed the sheets, but if this makes you more comfortable… we can change them, again."

SaeKu extended her arms, inviting Dade to drop the sheets in her hands. Shaking his head, he handed them to her. "I'll let you clean out the drawer. I'll change the sheets."

"That works." Dade shrugged, moving towards the dresser. "SaeKu."

He stopped in his tracks. "Yeah."

"I'm sorry, aight. I don't want you to think that any of this is intentional. Shit just keeps going left. I never plan to hurt your feelings or have you around here feeling like I'm your latest mistake."

"I know, Dade." SaeKu exclaimed.

"So what are we doing, SaeKu?" Dade asked. "You wit a nigga, or what?"

"I'm with you."

Chapter Nine

"Sage. I ain't that nigga Dade, and you sure as hell ain't SaeKu. This glock on my waist too heavy to be chasing your ass. Either you're coming down or I'm coming up... And if I have to come up, you'll regret that shit all night long. Now, bring your pretty ass on."

"Lorde. Go HOME!" Sage yelled through the phone, texting her new fling at the same time.

She'd met a decent guy while on her latest assignment, and wanted to see how things would go. Lorde was out of the question, but he wasn't getting it. It was after one in the morning, and he was making empty threats. There was no way that he would be able to get upstairs, so she wasn't worried about him coming up.

"You play too many fucking games, but I've got something for your ass." He ended the call, and Sage rejoiced. He'd been on the same shit all night long. It was as if he just didn't get it. Sage had counted him out just as quick as she'd counted him in.

After getting off the phone with Lorde, Sage prepared for her shower before bed. SaeKu had abandoned her, and she was left alone in their apartment. On nights like this, she wished that she had Pryce at her side.

Sage stepped out of the shower thirty minutes later, feeling refreshed in every way. She'd shampooed her hair, which she'd been needing to do for over a week. Time hadn't been on her side, but she was happy that she finally scratched it from her list.

Lorde crossed the dark street, being cautious of his surroundings. The small pink rag had been used as a receiving blanket for Pryce after she had a bottle. Shrugging, he brushed off the idea of being anything other than a love sick puppy. Sage was playing it tough, but he was tougher. She would be bringing her ass downstairs one way or another.

Once Lorde was up on her red Camry, he popped the gas tank, and stuck the blanket inside. It quickly became saturated with gasoline. Lorde cussed, mumbling, and going straight off on Sage as he pulled the lighter from his pocket, and lit the small cloth. Once it went up into flames, Lorde hurried across the street to his truck, and pulled further down the block.

Within seconds, there was a loud explosion, causing Lorde to burst into laughter. Sage's precious little ride had been blown to shreds, and was now on fire. Lorde exited his vehicle, and moved back in on the car –which was engulfed in flames. Pulling his cell out, he took five photos of the burning matter, one including a selfie. At once, he sent them all to Sage's cell.

I said come downstairs.

He sent a simple message with the photos. Within seconds, Lorde heard his name being called from upstairs. By now, a few people had come outside to watch the car burn to shreds. Looking up, he noticed Sage hanging out of the window of her apartment. Even in the dark, he could see the scowl on her beautiful face.

"What the fuck?" she yelled out.

Lorde shrugged with a smirk on his face. "You may want to come down and see this." He pointed at her car, which was still in flames.

"Oh my fucking gosh, nigga." She removed herself from the window, and shut it behind her. Within three minutes, she was walking up on Lorde full force.

"Oh shit." Lorde checked behind him before he started to walk backwards. He could sense the aggression radiating from Sage's body feet away. With his hands in the air, he tried blocking the punches that she was raining on his body.

"You're so fucking psychotic. Who would do something so stupid?" Sage was furious. Now, Lorde was beginning to think that he was a bit on the psychotic side, himself, but he didn't give a fuck. He was willing to do whatever it took for her to talk to him. If he had to trip the fire alarms in her building, then that was the next step. There weren't any boundaries to how far he was willing to go.

After she's had exhausted all of her energy, Lorde tucked her hands behind her back, and dove in for a kiss. "MOVE!" Sage yelled. "Crazy ass nigga!" she was so upset with him that she couldn't help but to cry.

"Why would you do that to my car?" she freed her hands and pointed at her car. "What is wrong with you, Lorde?" her tears made Lorde feel like shit. He hadn't meant to cause her an pain, but he needed her. She wasn't giving in to him any other way, so he tried a different route. He'd exercised all the general ones, but she wasn't leaving him much to work with.

"I needed to see you." He tried to get her to see his point of view, but that wasn't happening.

"This is not the way to do things Lorde. Maybe if you had let up, then I would've seen you eventually. This…" Sage pointed back at her car. "Is no way to get me to see things your way. This just shows me that I've made the right decision by not fucking with your ass. My car, though. Ugh!" Sage turned.

Before she could get far away, Lorde pulled her towards the side of the stoop they were near. "Listen. If this counts for anything, I was planning to buy you a new ride. I couldn't have my girl riding Camry while I could purchase any car that her heart desired. It was either set that bitch on fire or have it crushed. I just couldn't help myself tonight. In a few days, that car was going to be replaced, and you were supposed to walk out to a brand new G. I see how much you admire mine."

Lorde was pulling out all of the stops. Yes, he'd planned on upgrading Sage, but not so soon. He'd allowed his emotions to get the best of him. Now, he was stuck with his foot in his mouth.

"Lorde, it's best that you find a new hobby, because I'm not it. The little month that we've spent breathing down each other's neck is not worth a lifetime of horror stories." Sage wiped her tears, and got her act together.

"Almost two months. 6 weeks to be exact. That's how old baby girl is."

"What the fuck ever, Lorde. None of that really matters. I don't want shit that you have to offer. I'll file an insurance claim and get myself a new car. Stay the fuck away from me. If it doesn't have anything to do with Pryce, then leave me the hell alone."

"You know that I can't do that shit. You haven't even had a chance to suck my dick yet. I went down on you last time. Remember? You owe me one. Until then, I'm sticking my ass around. You can't just have a nigga going against the G code, then calling it off. You should've thought about that a long time ago."

"Oh my gosh. Are you serious right now?"

"Dead ass."

"You are so irky that it makes no sense. I swear… I wish I never laid eyes on your bald headed ass!"

"Ma'am. Is this your vehicle?" Sage and Lorde hadn't even noticed authorities had made their arrival. She figured the neighbors had called them, because she hadn't.

Rolling her eyes at Lorde, she turned to answer the officer who'd approached her. "Yes."

The fireman arrived on the scene, and began to put out the small fire that now existed.

"Do you have any clue as to how this happened?"

As much as Lorde hated the laws, he stepped up and began his speech. "Na, officer. If we knew, then we wouldn't be right here politicking with you. We came downstairs, and that bitch was near ashes." Lorde lied through his pearly white teeth.

"And no one saw anything? The officer questioned, writing in his pad.

"Officer, you hard of hearing?" Lorde asked.

"Excuse me?"

"Na. Ain't nobody see shit. Anymore questions?"

"I guess not, being that we need to find out the source of the fire before we can thoroughly investigate." The officer placed his pen in his shirt pocket. "You folks have a good night."

Sage and Lorde stood on the sidewalk, silently, as they watched fireman use hoses to cease the fire. The entire block had been blocked off while rescue workers performed their duties. When all was cleared out, Sage made her way back to her apartment.

"Where do you think you're going?" Sage questioned when she made it to the door of her building.

"What you mean?" Lorde chuckled, trying to play his shit cool.

"Lorde, you just burnt my fucking car to a crisp. You couldn't think that I was going to let you up like none of that happened."

"I thought we got over that, already."

"We haven't gotten over a damn thing."

"Yeah we did… Remember when I said I was getting you a new whip."

"So what?" Sage snatched her apartment building door open. "I don't need you to do anything but stay the hell away from me. I can get my own car, Lorde. You've totally outdone yourself."

"Okay. Okay. Damn. I'm sorry."

"Oh, I know." Sage stepped inside. "Have a nice life, Lorde."

"I fucked up!" Lorde concluded as he hopped the steps of Sage's apartments. As he made his way to his truck, he mentally prepared himself for the rollercoaster that he was about to be on. If Sage thought that she was leaving him, then she had another thing coming. There wasn't any backing out, and she needed to understand that.

**

"What did you get this time?" SaeKu leaned over Sage's shoulder to get a better view at her latest trinket.

Lorde wasn't missing a beat. Everyday for the last week, he had something new sent to their place. It started with flowers. Fruit were next. After that, the gifts began to get more lavish and expensive in taste. Her latest gift had come snapped around Pryce's neck. Sage hadn't noticed it until she removed her from her car seat. Since SaeKu had brought her up, she'd been chilling inside of it.

"A necklace from Tiffany's."

"Ah bitch, next it's going to be a rolex."

"He should really lay off."

"I mean… If you don't want it then I sure will take it."

"Girl, bye. I love this necklace. I'm just saying."

"What are you saying, exactly?" SaeKu questioned, sipping her tea. "Exactly," she replied when Sage couldn't supply her with an answer.

SaeKu's phone rung before Sage could reply to her statement. From the name on the screen, she could see that it was her baby. She and Dade had been trying their hardest to overcome every obstacle they'd been faced with, and connect with the beauty of their complicated union.

"Hey you." SaeKu answered.

"What you got going on?" Dade wanted to know.

"Nothing, about to get dressed for work."

"How long will yo be gone, again?"

"Two days. We went over this before I left this morning." True to his word, Dade was sure that he went to bed beside and woke up to SaeKu. It had been nights that he'd dreamt of this being his reality, but his wishing had finally come to fruition.

"What am I supposed to to for two whole days without the Queen in our castle?" Dade joked. "Slow down, yo!" he yelled in the background.

"Who are you talking to?" SaeKu laughed.

"Lorde. Let me call you back before this bummy ass nigga kill us both. He hasn't been giving a fuck since he got dumped. Tell Sage to give this man a chance before he end it all."

"Alright." SaeKu ended the call near tears. She was laughing so hard.

"Fuck you. Why did you just tell her that shit?" Lorde asked, zooming in and out of traffic. "I'm good."

"You convincing me or yourself? You've been on one since you dropped Pryce off. That girl got your head gone."

"It's that obvious, huh?"

"It is."

"Nigga… What if I'm in love?" Lorde looked over at Dade.

"Watch the road, don't watch me!" Dade yelled. "And it's too late for that. You're definitely in love."

"How do you know?" Lorde was new to this shit. Yeah, he'd felt something for Gia, but it was nothing compared to what he was feeling for Sage.

"Do your heart rate speed up at the thought of her?"

"Yeah." Lorde nodded.

"When you lay down at night, do you wish she was there beside you?"

"Yeah."

"When you wake up, do you wish you were sliding your morning hard into her soft and gushy?"

"Hell yeah." Lorde's face turned sour at the thought. Each morning, it was more of the same.

"Throughout the day, is she constantly on your mind?"

"Yeah."

"When you see niggas with their bitches, do that make you want to call her up?"

"Every time, but I'm still on block." Lorde sighed.

"Do you hate the thought of her being upset with you… making you want to do whatever it takes to get in her good graces?"

"Yeah. That's how I feel right now, but that ain't working." Lorde was frustrated with himself and Sage. They were meant, and he could feel it. If he could get her to look pass all that he'd done in the last few weeks, then they would be good.

"Well, my nigga. You're definitely in love."

"I am, huh?"

"Yeah." Dade nodded.

"Let me ask you something, though. How the fuck am I supposed to get her to overlook the shit I've been on lately?"

"You won't. You just have to make that shit up."

"I'm trying. That little motherfucker is stubborn as ever, though."

"Tell her."

"Tell her?" Lorde questioned.

"Yeah. Tell her what you just told me."

"What? That I love her?"

"Yeah, that… And the fact that this is new for you and you're trying to figure out the right shit to do, but it only equates to more fuck ups on your end." Dade coached. "Be honest, my nigga. It'll get you out of more shit than you think."

"Maybe you're right."

"SaeKu has a flight later on. Since you burnt the damn girl's car up, she's taking SaeKu to the airport so that she and Pryce will be able to get around."

"Man, I should've never did that. Look how she treats baby girl. She act like Pryce is hers. She even told me to ask Gia to sign over her rights."

"You should." Dade agreed. "Mama would tell you to do the same thing."

"You're right." Lorde nodded.

"But, that's your chance right there. Be waiting outside of her spot when she gets back. Air your shit out, and let her decide what she wants to do."

"What if it doesn't work?"

"Then don't stop trying until you're certain that this isn't something that she wants. Judging by the way that she is avoiding you… I think you're all good. Women only do that so that won't end up giving in. That only means she's still interested. If not, she wouldn't even bother blocking your number. She could tell you to go fuck yourself and never feel any type of way about it. If she really wanted out, then seeing your name pop up across her screen wouldn't mean shit to her. It does. That's why she doesn't want that bitch popping up." Dade laughed. "SaeKu have a nigga on block more than a little bit. I know, B. Trust me. I know."

**

Lorde sat outside of Sage's apartments, smoking blunt after blunt. His nerves were getting the best of him as he waited for her arrival. Thirty minutes into his wait, she appeared like a breath of fresh air after nearly drowning in sorrows. Lorde's heart smiled at the sight of her running around to the opposite side of the car to get his baby girl.

At that moment, he exited his truck, and ran to assist her. He had no intentions of scaring her, but he had. Her hand flew to her chest as she looked back at him with a scowl on her face. Lorde lifted his hands in the air in surrender.

"I come in peace." He muttered.

"What is it, Lorde?"

"Can we talk?"

"Five minutes. Don't take too long, because my little bug is hungry."

Lorde felt warm on the inside at her claiming Pryce as her own. "TALK!" she yelled, bringing him back to current.

"Can we go inside?"

"Na. We're good right here. What's up?"

"I don't know what I'm doing wrong." Lorde admitted. "I'm a street nigga that likes hood bitches. If we ain't fucking, we beefing in the streets. If we aren't beefing in the streets, then I'm handing out hush money to keep em quiet. That's all I know. That's all it's ever been." Lorde looked into Sage's eyes as he spoke to her. "But you switched up the game on me. I hadn't time to adjust."

"Maybe that's just what you need, Lorde. We can be friends, but I'm just not one of them."

"I know you're not. That's exactly why I'm trying. Have you been getting your gifts?"

"Yes. As nice as they are, that does not erase the damage that you've done."

"I understand that. I'm just out here trying. At least give me that."

"I'll give you that."

"What's next?"

"What do you mean what's next?" Sage asked.

"I mean… I'm running out of ideas. What am I to do next? My thoughts lead to fuck ups, so tell me what I've got to do to get you back on my team?"

"Give me time." Sage pulled Pryce's seat from the car. "Let me breathe."

"That's a lot to ask, Sage." Lorde admitted. He bent down to pull the blanket from his daughter's face. She was looking up at him, and began to kick and squirm when she saw his smile.

"You've got her spoiled rotten, Lorde."

"That's all you." Lorde held his hands up. "I just try to keep up."

"Whatever," Sage chuckled. "I have to get her upstairs. "Maybe I'll see you around."

"Can you take my phones off of block." He questioned, grabbing Pryce's car seat from her arms so that he could walk them to the door.

"You're really aiming high, here." Sage smirked.

"I just thought that I'd try." Lorde found solace in her answer. If Lorde was right then that was a sign of good faith.

"Try again next time." Sage laughed.

As they made it to the door, Lorde handed Sage Pryce's car seat. He was careful not to try and force himself onto Sage or get her to allow him upstairs. He hadn't come on no funny shit. Lorde simply wanted to talk.

"Sage." Lorde mustered up a mound of strength from some unknown source. Pulling the trigger on a fuck boy had required less courage than what Lorde was about to do.

"Yeah." Sage held the door open, and turned back.

"I think I'm in love with you." He dropped his head as the words rolled off of his tongue.

"You think?" Sage asked as her eyes glossed over.

“I know it.” Lorde found the audacity to continue. “You know it.” He pointed between the two of them. “I’m working on the showing it part, but can you please cut me some slack. What you want from me? It’s yours.”

“Time, Lorde. I need time.”

With that, Sage went inside, leaving Lorde with his thoughts. If time was what she wanted, then time was what she’d get. He couldn’t promise how much time he would give her, but he would step off for a second. Even with their brief encounter, he felt like they’d made some sort of progress. His smile was wide as the Nile River as he journeyed back to his truck. He fist pumped once he got inside, promising to front Dade the baddest stripper in Aces when they went the following night.

Chapter Ten

Things with Sage and Lorde had gotten a little less rocky since they'd last saw one another. As she had requested, he was giving her time to consider. They'd both come up with a schedule for Pryce's visits to Sage's, which worked in both of their favor. However, they had yet to speak to one another. The tension had dissipated, but the urgency was still present on Lorde's end.

Sage continued her routine of having Lorde to drop Pryce off at Dade's place for SaeKu to bring her home, or SaeKu would go downstairs to meet him. While time was on her side, Sage felt the need to explore more options. She wasn't about to jump into some relationship, but she was really feeling her new friend guy. He was the total opposite of Lorde, which was what she needed in her life. She'd summed up the fact that she wasn't about that trap queen shit. Her life was too simple to try and complicated it all of a sudden.

"Has he called, yet?" Sage questioned SaeKu.

"No. I told you to just call him."

"That man does not have it all. If I call him, then he will think that it means something more than what it really does."

"Well, I'll just stay with her until he comes. It's no biggie. Go ahead and go on your date. What I will say is that you should hurry before he just pops up. If you're downstairs when he comes… Girl." SaeKu laughed. "I feel for you, honey."

"That nigga is crazy as fuck, huh? Like… How is that level of craziness even humanly possible?"

"Right." SaeKu shook her head. "I don't know what you're going to do about him. You can't avoid him forever."

"I'm hoping some thot comes along and sweep him off of his feet."

"Na. He knows what it feels like to be in the presence of a real woman, now. That can never be replaced by some tramp. You've got that nigga head gone." SaeKu warned. "He's in it for the long haul."

"I hope he gives up soon."

"I doubt it. He talks Dade's ear off about you every day."

"Oh Lord."

"Exactly."

"Well, let me finish up with my makeup, and then I am out of here."

Sage had made plans, and she wasn't going to allow Lorde to fuck them up. She was going on a date with her little boo, and she was excited. Even with Lorde's antics, she'd placed her problems with him on the backburner. One monkey didn't stop her show. He'd shown how delusional he was, and Sage wasn't willing to put up with the shit.

Of course she wouldn't allow Pryce to suffer, which is why she continued to get her whenever she was off. With her parents being dead, Sage didn't really have anyone. For the same reasons that Lorde had decided to claim her as his own, Sage used to keep her around.

They were both missing that family structure that they craved, both hungry for that unconditional love that parents and siblings offered. Lorde had Dade, but Sage had nothing. Of course, SaeKu loved her to death, but it was just different. They hadn't grown up together, or suffered much of anything.

Sage was thankful of their friendship, and SaeKu offering her family for Sage to consider her own, but she still felt like something was missing. Unknowingly, Pryce was her fulfillment. It was the main reason she craved her company.

**

"Hey uncle baby!" Dade stood over Pryce, cooing.

She was the prettiest child he'd ever laid eyes on. Her brown skin and near red hair was all a result of her trifling ass mother. For once, she'd done good for herself. Dade hissed at the thought of shit Lorde told him that she had pulled.

Seeing Pryce made him wonder what the new baby would look like. Although he knew that Alani should've been the last thing on his mind, she wasn't. He'd broken things off with her, but wanted to know how she was holding up during the last stretch of her pregnancy. In a few weeks, the baby was due, and he knew she must be scared out of her mind.

"You hear that?" Dade questioned. "You hear that noise? That's your rude ass pops blasting his trap music in my driveway. I'm going to leave him sitting out there a minute longer just for pulling that shit." Dade used baby talk to explain the madness going on outside of his door. "Yes I am. Yes I am."

He had been put on baby duty while SaeKu went to shower. He didn't mind, though. He loved the brief visits from Pryce. She was the perfect child. She never gave anyone any problems. She would sit in her car seat for hours, and never cry out or make many noises. She'd just stare at the bright colored toys that dangled from her handle.

As expected, Lorde came banging on the door like he was the fucking laws. Dade simply ignored him, and continued to play with Pryce. "Dade. Don't you hear your crazy ass cousin knocking?" SaeKu came downstairs in the silk robe that Dade had purchased her a few days prior.

"Girl, if you don't get your ass back up there in that robe."

Dade chastised, stopping SaeKu in her tracks. He'd gotten the robe for personal reasons that he everything to do with easy access and sex appeal. When SaeKu wore that robe, it was for no ones eyes but his. Besides, he had some shit he needed to tell Lorde.

"I saw you standing right there the entire fucking time, yo." Lorde fumed.

Laughing, Dade stepped aside, and let him in. "Hey to your rude ass, too. Did you call that number?"

"Yeah. The nigga Loco picked up. That young buck kept the phone charged that fucking long. He's serious about getting his paper, though. I know an animal when I see one."

"Yeah. I peeped that too." Dade handed Lorde Pryce's diaper bag, and her car seat.

"Good looking, bro."

"No problem." Dade checked his surroundings before leaning in, and whispering to Lorde. "She's on a date."

His face contorted as he allowed Dade's words to sink in. Without hesitation, he handed Dade back Pryce's diaper bag, and sat her car seat on the floor. Dipping down, he removed her, and hugged her small body.

"Daddy missed you little worm." He rubbed in Pryce's hair. She was all gums as she smiled at her old man. "I have a run to make and a bitch to check."

"Lorde. Really, B?"

"That's how I'm feeling my G. Keep an eye on little mama. See if you can get me a location on Sage. She's got the game fucked up… I swear. I'm going to have to break all of her fucking legs just to get her to sit down and try with me."

"Why do I believe every word you're saying right now. Chill out, dog. You're slick possessive."

"Na. She ain't even over me yet. How the hell she going to be on to the next nigga. She got me out here looking like a fucking clown while she's making other plans and shit."

"I feel you. I'd do the same if SaeKu ever tried that with me. I'll try to snatch up SaeKu's line. They share their location 24/7."

"Aight. I'm out of here, mama." Lorde kissed his daughter's cheek, and handed her to Dade. "Y'all mind keeping her for the night? I ain't trying to come back."

"She's in good hands. SaeKu needs some practice, anyway."

"You ain't bout that life, nigga. Don't front."

"We'll see."

Lorde's patience was running thin. It had been weeks since he'd last spoken to Sage, and he missed her like crazy. His ashtray was filling by the minute, due to the chain he'd started. However, it wasn't cigarettes that he was toking. He'd been busting down blunts since he parked next to the two door BMW with the white guts.

His call from Dade about an hour ago had him on edge, and nothing about the message he sent was sitting well with him. It was the exact reason he was stationed where he was at the moment. On one hand he felt like a deranged stalker. Yet, on the other, he felt as if his actions were justified. Sage had put something on him, entangling him in her web of mystery. She was different, much different.

Nothing about her mirrored the women that he was used to dating. She was soft by nature, a pure sweetheart. However, she didn't put up with his shit. Sage wasn't the confrontational type that he usually liked. She would cut a nigga off in a heartbeat, and that shit got to Lorde. He was accustomed to women wanting to go to war for him.

Sage wasn't waging war. The only battle that she was willing to fight was the one to protect her heart. With Gia's antics at the forefront of their budding relationship, Lorde had lost Sage before he could get a good grip on her.

This situation was different, though. Lorde had grown fond of dropping hoes like flies, but, evidentially, this wasn't the case. Like a thief in the night, Sage had stolen something from Lorde that he didn't know he was willing to give –his heart. She'd dug her claws into his beet read vessel and marked her territory.

Lorde's dark skin discolored itself, deepening as if he'd been baking in the European sun for days. In fact, his body felt the effects of the scolding hot rays as he witnessed Sage emerging from the five-star diner with her hands entrapped with another. Her amazingly beautiful smile shined, even in the dark of the night, tearing away at Lorde's manhood. In his mind, it was his duty to bring her sheer joy and pleasure in such a way that kept her gleaming with joy. No other man was supposed to take parts in the cause. It was completely out of the question.

Throwing the cigar and weed crumbles that he was meshing together in the ashtray, Lorde pulled the handle to his door. Snatching it open, he tugged at the blunt that rested between his lips. Clouds of smoke filled the air, as he positioned himself on the hood of his car. His jeans hung slightly off of his ass, in a very tasteful manner. Both his pistol and his money were at a tug of war, threatening to outweigh each other. While the knot in either pocket kept his jeans snug, the pistol made promises to pull them lower.

"So this what you do when you mad at a nigga?"

"LORDE?" Sage was astounded at his presence.

Stopping midstride, she turned to Toliver with sympathetic eyes. They'd just enjoyed an evening of fine dinning, laughs, and corny jokes. It was embarrassing to be met by Lorde's rashness after such a delightful time.

"Don't Lorde me. A nigga ain't even did shit, personally, and you're already on to the next."

"Lorde, I'm not going to do this with you." Sage blew out in frustration.

"Bullshit. You're going to do this wherever the fuck I want to. I've tried the cynic route, and that shit didn't work."

"So you decide to show up while she's on a date?" Sage's date butted in, pissing Lorde off. He was looking for a reason to put his ass flat on his back.

"Hey Arnold, ain't nobody asked your ass shit. Seems to me you should be thankful that I didn't come inside. Keep yapping and this shit can get as ugly as that over aged pimple on your fucking cheek."

"Lorde. Please. Go home. I've told you that we have nothing to discuss, and I think that you should consider the fact that you're mimicking a deranged stalker right now."

"See, the difference is… I ain't chasing after no motherfucker that doesn't want to be caught. You may be fooling yourself, but you ain't fooling me."

Lorde was outraged at the fact that Sage had prettied herself of for the likes of another man. She was stunning in her evening gown and polished face. Her hair hug past her shoulders, and neared her butt. The highlights that she'd gotten earlier that day complimented her brown skin tone very well.

"You're insane." Sage yelled.

"Call it how you see it. I just go all out for mine."

"Lorde. Go home."

"Not unless you're coming with me."

"Excuse me? Come with you? Are you nuts? Why did I ask that? Of course you are!" Sage threw her hand in the air. "Because what sane person would set a fucking car on fire just because they felt like it."

“I told you that I’m sorry about that, and that wasn’t the reason.” Lorde shrugged, pulling from his blunt. “The real reason was because you didn’t want to come downstairs. That was the only way I could get you down there.”

“I swear… You’re insane. Where is Pryce?” Sage’s mind drifted to the beautiful baby girl that she’d grown to love. Being that Lorde was standing before her, she couldn’t help but to question Pryce’s whereabouts.

“Home, where you need to be!”

“How is she at home? Who is she with at home?” The questions started flying from Sage’s lips. She was beginning to sound like a concerned mother, and Lorde was sounding like a scorn baby father.

“She’s in good hands. But fuck all of that. Let’s roll.” Lorde knew that his baby girl was good, so he wasn’t worried. However, Sage was pissing him off more and more by the minute.

“I’m not going with you. Come on Toliver.” Sage grabbed Toliver’s hand, and pulled him towards his car.

Chuckling, Lorde lifted from his hood, and went for his waistline. He pulled out his pistol, and aimed it. “Sage, let ole boy go, and come on.”

Sage looked back to see the gun pointed, and became furious. “Put that shit away, maniac.”

“Yo, Sage… Let’s go.” Toliver grabbed Sage’s attention, tugging her in the direction of his car..

Lorde stared daggers into her, wondering what decision she was about to make. His heart split into pieces when she sighed and turned back towards the BMW that Lorde had been parked next to.

"Sage, move." Lorde yelled before dumping.

BOOM.

The first window shattered.

BOOM.

Then there was the second.

BOOM.

The third window was closest to him.

BOOM.

The forth one was to follow.

He nearly emptied his clip into Toliver's ride. Knowing that he had a bit more ammunition, he began to aim for Toliver's feet. The spark on the ground, and closeness of the bullets had Toliver playing hopscotch to doge the flesh seeking pieces of lead. By the time he was done dancing and skipping, he was upon his ride. Pulling the door open, he hopped inside, and sped off. He didn't give a fuck how Sage got home. His life was more valuable than any relationship that he was trying to pursue.

"What is it with you and cars?" Sage stomped away.

Tucking his gun inside of his jeans, Lorde turned in her direction. "They are the only way to get to you I guess."

"That was so uncalled for. You're some type of animal. Why don't you just leave me alone." Sage huffed, tired of the drama that Lorde was bringing to her doorstep. "I don't like this shit, Lorde. If this is the way that you plan to win over a girl like me, then you're doing it all wrong."

"Tell me what to do, then? Shit, at least a nigga trying. Tell me what I've got to do, Sage, because I ain't letting you dance off in the sun with another nigga. That's not happening."

"And that's not fair. You come with too much. I can't handle the stuff that you bring to the table. Quite frankly, I don't even know if it's worth it, Lorde."

"Na. How the fuck do you call it fair to put that little pussy on a nigga like that and then try to take that shit back? As long as I'm alive, I'm the only one dipping in and breathing on that motherfucker. I'm telling you, Sage. Don't play with me. I'm trying to be cool, and you out here buggin." Lorde couldn't believe himself, either.

He'd lost his whole top in a matter of seconds. Thinking that Sage had chosen the next nigga over him had him ready to set flames to the city. He figured this was what niggas were referring to when they said motherfuckers was ready to lose it all when it came to their bitch.

"I'm not doing this with you." Sage took off in the opposite direction.

"Good, because I don't want you to." Lorde countered. He ran around to the passenger side of his car, and snatched the door open. Grabbing the contents of the passenger seat, he slammed the door, and ran up behind Sage. "But, you gone walk the soles off of them red bottoms trying to make it home." Lorde chuckled.

Sage couldn't contain the giggles that fell from her lips. She was upset, but Lorde always found a way to make things better. Turning around, sensing his presence, she lifted her hand to slap him across the chest. Midair, her hand halted and fell to her very own chest.

"Lorde." She gasped. "They're beautiful."

"I would assume. They cost a nigga a grip." Lorde pulled his pants up with his free hand, and extended his other to hand Sage the box of deep red roses that he'd gotten her.

"I don't understand you. You just…"

"Speaking of that, I need to be out. You hear them sirens? We ain't in the jects. Theses bitches hear gunshots, and they calling twelve. You rolling or you walking the red off them bottoms?"

"I can't stand you!" Sage walked around Lorde, and but turned back to ask a question.

"You really love a nigga. Don't front." He grabbed his dick through his jeans in an attempt to calm himself down.

"Why do you have to do all of this, Lorde?" She was actually curious. He wasn't going down without a fight. She didn't know whether to be scared or appreciative.

"I don't know. I'm just going for what I want." He shrugged.

"This isn't the way to do it." Sage leaned her head to the side, and rubbed her hand through her hair.

"How you going to give another man a chance, and you won't even give me one."

"I did! You just keep messing up." She reminded him.

"Not really. I'm still trying to fix what I messed up the first time."

"By constantly messing up more."

"Well, whose fault does that sound like."

"Man! Whatever." Sage turned and stomped to the car.

Lorde stayed behind for a brief second, trying to pinpoint the condition of his mind. He was buying flowers, shooting at niggas, and craving companionship like never before. Sage was something special, as his mother would say. Looking up to the sky, he made a silent promise to his mother and God to do right by this lovely soul. Even the contemplation of losing her caused too much chaos in his chest.

"Where are we going?" Sage asked, fixing her lipstick in the mirror. As much as she wished that she'd kept walking, she knew it wasn't an option. Lorde had her right where he wanted her. Besides, he would've stayed around rather the cops were on the way or not. The last thing she wanted was for him to be sitting behind bars.

"To eat."

"I just left from a da…"

"I triple dog dare you to remind me of that shit back there." Lorde barked. "Since you want to go out and shit, then that's what we're doing. Next time a date crosses your mind, I need to be the next thought."

"Whatever."

"Aight."

Rolling her eyes into the top of her head, Sage sighed. Ten minutes into their ride, she felt heat echoing from Lorde's body. As he neared her, Sage's heart swelled. Grabbing her hand, Lorde intertwined his fingers with hers, keeping his eyes on the road.

His dark skin blushed as Sage tightened her grip. Completely out of his element, Lorde was smitten the connection that he and Sage shared. The way that she pushed his dope dealings to the back of his mental was rewarding. When with her, none of that shit matter.

Looking down at Lorde's meaty fingers, Sage smiled. He was the roughest teddy bear that she'd ever encountered. Even with his tough exterior, she knew that he meant well. There was no doubt in her mind that he loved hard. In fact, he was going to bat just to make sure that he was given the same in return.

To some degree, she was willing to admit that she loved him as well. Even with his fucked up ways, there was so much more to who he was. She knew that he needed love. With the loss of his mother and the trifling ass bitch for a baby mother, Sage was his only hope for a normal functioning relationship. She figured she'd better put on her knee pads and helmet, because she was in it for the long ride.

Chapter Eleven

"This was not apart of the agreement." Sage frowned.

"You acting like I'm dipping out on you. I've paid my half of the rent up for the remainder of our lease. You're good." SaeKu continued to fold her clothes. "It's not like I'm really moving in. I'm taking some things, but I will be back and forth. I don't think that I'm ready to actually be there full time. Being there is just a little more convenient for me."

"To do what? Because the airport is closer to our place. What's it convenient for? Rolling over to the dick?" Sage was throwing a hole pound of shade at SaeKu.

"You're sounding like a real hater. Maybe if you came down from your high horse, you wouldn't be deprived."

"I don't know what you're talking about."

"Girl, please. You've got that man walking on pins and needles."

"He needs it. He's been out of line since day one. I have to show that nigga who is boss. As long as he's on that bullshit, then he won't be getting any."

"Whatever. I heard you shaving this morning. As soon as I'm out of the door, you're calling him up to go jump his bones."

"Damn, you know me so well." Sage admitted. "But I was at least going to wait until tonight. He's taking me to dinner."

"Well, I sure as hell hope y'all have found a sitter, because I am not fucking around with Pryce, tonight. My man and I are getting some alone time."

"The nerve of you heffas. It's cool, though. His mother's friend has agreed to sit for Pryce five days out of the week. The other two, I'm off, so we have everything under cover. We tacked on today as an add on. She doesn't mind, though. She'd old. She's bored, and she never had kids of her own."

"Well, that's the perfect match."

"Right. She keeps Pryce on point. She even put them pig tails in her head that she was rocking the other day."

"Those were too cute."

"I know."

"Whatever you do, don't forget that the crew is coming up tomorrow. We've planned lunch and shopping, so free yourself."

"That goes without saying." Sage was excited to see everyone. She was sure to get a laugh or two out of the girls pertaining to her current situation. Lorde was a hot mess, and everyone found it comical but her.

"Well, I'm out of here kid. I'll see you in the morning." SaeKu pulled the handles on the suitcases that she'd packed to take over Dade's house.

"Alright. Lock up behind you. I don't feel like moving."

**

After what felt like a million errands, SaeKu was finally turning the key that Dade had given her earlier that morning. Opened the door to find the house pitch black. Sighing, she dropped the bags in the foyer, and pulled out her cell. Dade had promised they could stay in and watch movies until they both fell asleep. However, he was nowhere in sight.

As his phone rung, SaeKu begin to smile. She could hear it in the distance, meaning that he was inside as promised. SaeKu ended the call, picked her bags up, and walked deeper into the house. As she got closer to the living room, candles appeared –directing her towards the kitchen instead. When she made it to the space designated for dinners and beyond, SaeKu gasped.

Dade was standing near the stove, with a bottle of Champagne in his hand. "How was your day, beautiful?" Dade's words poured a pound more of love into her body. She was always hungry for more.

"It was so so until I walked in the kitchen to find you here." SaeKu smiled. "I hadn't even noticed the aroma until, now. You cooked?"

"Do you see anyone else here that could've?"

"Maybe you ran them off before I came."

"I didn't know when I should be expecting you, so that wouldn't have worked."

"What do you have up your sleeve?" SaeKu squinted her eyes. "Candles. Roses." She smelled the fresh batch in front of her. "And food. What's the occasion?"

"You finally stopped giving me a hard time. That's worth celebrating, right?" Dade raised a brow.

"I guess you can say that."

"Plus."

"Plus?" SaeKu questioned.

"I have an important meeting out of state, so I'll be gone for a few days. I wanted to spend some time with you before I took off."

"So, that's the deal?" SaeKu rolled her eyes.

"Don't be that way."

"I thought I was going to be able to spend the rest of my off days with you."

"I'll be back before you know it."

"And I'll be on a plane to the next city."

"We can't worry about that right now. Let's just focus on tonight. Go wash your hands so that I can feed you, woman."

"Be right back." SaeKu cheered up, not wanting to ruin the mood, but she was super salty about what Dade had just threw on her. For the next few days, she would probably lock herself inside of the house.

When SaeKu returned downstairs, Dade had plated their food, and was waiting for her at the table. She sat, and the two prayed together. As dinner commenced, the two begin to converse.

"I'm so happy, Dade." SaeKu voiced.

"As you should be."

"No. You don't understand. I've been avoiding this feeling for so long. It hasn't been for reasons everyone might think, but simply because I feel like when you're all the way up… You fall so much harder. I've been afraid of falling. That's why I was running from all of this." SaeKu waved around. "It just puts me all the way up there, and I never want to come down."

"You never have to." Dade spoke to her soul. "I've only ever wanted what was best for you. I seen something so genuine in your eyes. I hadn't sought out a woman's presence since the day I first touched a sack of dope, and that was forever ago. I didn't give a fuck about loving a woman. Hell, the woman that birthed me taught me all I needed to know about women, but you changed that. You had me thinking differently."

"Reed told me that she had someone she wanted me to meet. However, you saw me before she could make the connection."

"Reed. That's my nigga. She was looking out for a nigga, and I still owe her big time for that."

"They'll be here in the morning."

"I know." Dade had a slip of the tongue.

"How'd you know?"

"I employ her husband, baby. How wouldn't I know when the misses were visiting the hometown?"

"Right." SaeKu forked her veggies before stuffing them into her mouth.

"Y'all got anything planned?" Dade was curious.

"Yeah. We're meeting for lunch. Besides that, nothing. Of course we may do a little shopping, but that's about it."

"Aight. I'll leave you some paper just incase y'all do decide."

"Thanks babe." SaeKu smiled.

She was finding herself falling head over heels for Dade. At a point, she didn't even think it was humanly possible. However, he was winning her over a bit more as each day passed. He was so perfect that SaeKu, nearly, thought that their thing was too good to be true. But, he continued to remind her that this was the real thing.

As she grew to accept it, she grew to accept all of the struggles she's encountered to get to this point. Everything seemed worth it, all of a sudden. As she sat at the dinner table, across from the love of her life, nothing in life seemed unworthy. Everything that had happened, had to happen. That's the way she saw it, and that's the way it was.

Both Dade and SaeKu enjoyed their quiet dinner together. After a night of straight fucking, the two drifted off in one another's arms. SaeKu was filled with so much happiness that she even woke with a smile. However, it quickly disappeared after realizing she'd woke to an empty bed. As promised, Dade had left her some cash, replacing himself with the doe. On his side of the bed was note, with the cash right next to it.

Had to run, early. Enjoy yourself.

SaeKu's frown was turned upside down, immediately. She grabbed the cash from his side of the bed, and dumped it all into her purse. Checking the clock, she realized she'd overslept.

Her meeting with the girls was in a little over an hour. She, quickly, dressed, and was out of the door just in time to still make lunch.

When SaeKu walked into Breadwinners, the crew were still waiting to be seated. Everyone in attendance was all smiles, except for Reed. She tapped her foot, impatiently as they waited to be called back. As SaeKu's eyes traveled the length of her body, she acknowledged the source of her attitude. She was definitely expecting.

"I guess you ladies were right." SaeKu pointed at Reed's growing belly.

"Hell yeah. She knew damn well Keem had knocked her up. Now, she's walking around with an attitude like it's everybody fault but hers." Belly rolled her eyes into the top of her head.

"So, yall just going to talk about me like I'm not standing right here?" Reed interfered.

"Because no one has time for all of that attitude you're dishing out."

"I'm good. I don't have an attitude."

"Well, why is your face screwed up?" Kelly questioned.

"My face screwed up?" Reed dug threw her purse to find her compact mirror.

"This heffa been looking so mean lately that she doesn't even realize she's looking like a hard ass half the time." Bella shook her head as they were called to be seated.

"Where's Sage?" SaeKu started to look around. "She should be here by now."

"We thought she was tagging along with you."

"No, I left from Dade's to get here."

"Okaaaaaaaaaaaay!" Bella high-fived SaeKu. "That's the shit I'm talking about."

"Little baby came back and got her man." Kelly whistled as they walked to their seats.

"Not really. He wouldn't let up… Like… Not at all." SaeKu blushed. "But I'm happy he didn't."

“I bet.” Bella smiled. “I know good dick when I see it. It be written all over a bitch’s face.”

“Oh hush up!” SaeKu shied away from the topic.

“It is what it is. How you think I got three bad heathens, Bella has two… And Reed… Well.” Kelly shrugged. “You get the point.” Everyone at the table burst out laughing at Reed’s expense.

“Y’all ain’t right.” Reed flicked them off.

“Are you guys ready to order your drinks?” the waitress appeared.

“We will all take waters to start. Don’t rush back, we will be a minute.” Bella informed their waitress.

“Okay. I’ll have those waters right out.”

“Anyway.” Kelly started. “What’s been up in your world?”

“Nothing much. I’ve been working my ass off, basically. Besides that, I’ve been using my free time to work on whatever this thing is that Dade and I have going on.”

“Well, you look pretty damn happy.” Bella smiled.

“I am.” SaeKu admitted.

“I’ve been running away from this for forever, and I can’t even really say why.”

“You needed time, that’s all.” Bella knew the struggle. “We all understood.”

“I bet you guys thought I was foolish.”

“No, we thought you were young, and you were. We couldn’t force anything down your throat. When the time was right, we knew it would happen.” Kelly stated.

“We all knew.” Reed agreed. “It was too obvious not to see the connection.”

"Hey y'all. What's good?" Sage stepped into the vicinity looking like new money.

"Check you out!" Bella started, and the team followed up.

"Looking like fresh money."

"All done up and shit." Kelly clapped. "Yassssss. What these New York niggas doing to my girls?"

"I don't know, but I like it." Reed high-fived Bella.

"Y'all so with it." Sage pulled a chair out, and sat.

"I thought you would be here before me."

"I would've, but I had an impromptu meeting."

"With who?"

"Dade." SaeKu nearly choked off of her spit. The last she'd heard, Dade was off to another city.

"Excuse me."

"He wanted me to give you these." Sage dug into her purse and gathered flight information and passport that Dade had given her.

"What?" SaeKu's hands covered her mouth. She reached out and grabbed the flight itinerary, searching for the destination, but there wasn't one. "Where are we going?"

"I don't know." Sage shrugged. "He said that you'd have to see when you got there. He's waiting on you."

"Wait. Now?"

"Yeah. You see the time?" Sage pointed to the departure time on the itinerary that she'd just given. "That's in an hour."

"But I haven't packed." SaeKu became frantic at the thought of packing and making it to the private strip in time for take off.

"Already covered. He's supplying you with new gear for the entire trip."

"Baby, if you don't shut up with all of these questions, and get your ass up!" Bella pushed SaeKu forward.

"Oh my God. This man…" SaeKu begin to tear up as she grabbed her belongings, and started to make her exit. "He just keeps getting better with time."

"We've all been through it." Kelly smiled. "Falling in love is amazing, isn't it."

"It is!" SaeKu kissed each of the girl's cheeks, wiping her tears as she ditched their date to go be with her man. As she walked out of the restaurant, her emotions unfolded. She cried the entire way to her car. This was it. Dade was everything that she could've imagined, and so much more.

SaeKu was a mess by the time she made it to the strip. Her eyes were puffy and her nose was red. She didn't have time to open her door before someone was at her side. "Thanks." She didn't neglect her manners as she was ushered to the private jet before her.

The thin strip of carpet met her heels as she made her way to her beloved Dade. Step by step, she climbed, waiting for the moment that she saw his face. As expected, he was looking like the biggest boss as he sat with one leg over the other. His hands were folded in front of him, as he stared off into space. At the notion of her arrival, Dade stood to his feet, and greeted her with a smile.

"Good morning, SaeKu."

"Well, hello. Aren't you a little sneaky something."

"I just thought it would be better if you didn't know." Dade shrugged. "You ready?"

"Ready as I'll ever be."

"Good."

"Where are we going?"

"To some land far far away." Dade spoke. "To a place called Bella Island."

SaeKu had heard wonderful stories from Reed and Bella about how beautiful the lands was that RahMeek had purchased for Bella. She'd wanted to visit, but had no intentions on going unless the family had invited her. Now, she was going to be spending the rest of her off days on the island with her man and that was even better.

SaeKu sat next to Dade, and strapped herself in. Once he was seated and the cabin door was locked, she placed her hand inside of his, and leaned her head onto his shoulder. Before the captain could even announce their footage, she had dozed off.

Chapter Twelve

"Where are you taking me?" Each day, Lorde was showing Sage the better half of him.

Under difference circumstances and with a different person, Sage would've found it to be romantic to have been blind folded. With Lorde, things were truly unpredictable. She couldn't tune into the romantic side of things for the simple fact that she was too concerned with what she'd be faced with after the cloth was pulled from her eyes.

"You've asked the same question three times. You're running my patience raggedy. I'm about to say fuck this shit and send your ass into traffic if you don't shut the hell up." Lorde barked.

Chuckling, Sage shook her head. "It's just against the law for you to keep your cool, huh?"

"Stay right here." Lorde positioned Sage, and dared her to move. "Don't move."

He ran back to his truck, and pulled a small blanket that belonged to Pryce out of the back. The burping cloth was fresh out of the pack, so he felt like it wouldn't hurt to use it. Jogging back towards Sage, he said, "Open up."

"What?" she asked, incredulously.

"Open your mouth!"

"Why would I be…"

Before she could finish her statement, Lorde had stuffed the cloth inside of her mouth. "Now, that'll get you to keep that big ass mouth of yours closed. You're about to ruin the surprise and shit."

Lorde bent over in laughter at the obscenities that Sage was more than likely spitting under the cloth, but he couldn't hear her. Snatching her arm, he pulled her down the walkway, near her home. When they made it to their destination, he untied the silk cloth from her eyes, and smiled.

"That's all you." He pointed at the truck that was in front of them. He pulled the cloth from her mouth and allowed her to speak. The entire time, he'd been holding her hands so she couldn't touch either.

"NO!" She exclaimed. "You didn't. Did you?"

"I did!" Lorde was filled with joy at the sight of Sage's smile. He'd been fucking up so much that he was happy to have gotten something right for once.

"Oh my GOD!" Sage jumped on Lorde and begin to rain kisses all over his face. She paid no mind to the pedestrians when she felt his dick harden. She maneuvered her body up and down, with his hands resting on her ass.

"Don't start shit out here. I'll bend you over that stoop over there, and we'd both get arrested for indecent exposure." Lorde put Sage down, and ran his hand over the length of his dick, attempting to get it to calm down.

"A G Wagon, though."

"I needed my lady to match my fly."

"Your lady?" Sage rolled her eyes into the top of her head.

"Damn right. I've spent $200,000 on the truck and customization. Damn right. You OFFICIALLY became my lady once I handed the money over to them niggas."

"I love the color. What made you get it sprayed like this?"

"I knew that was your favorite."

Lorde had gotten a layer of lavender with glittered specks painted on the truck. It wasn't too dark or too light. It was perfect in Sage's eyes.

"I can't believe this."

"Well, believe it, then. I've been on some other shit, but I'm done with that. I talked to God for the first time since my mother left this earth, and he told me this is it. So, who am I to defy that man. I just need for you to tell me that you're willing to give me that chance I've been begging for."

"You've got your chance, Lorde. Don't mess it up."

Rejoicing, Lorde picked Sage's small body up into the air, and spun her around. He was happier than a kid in an amusement park with unlimited tickets to ride everything their heart desired. "I swear I won't. Come take a look inside of your whip."

Lorde carried Sage to the truck, and placed her inside of it. She played with the gadgets and got acquainted with her sound system. Lorde had the original one removed and replaced it with one just like his. He'd even put speakers in the trunk, and threw some rims on to replace the manufactured tires. Her truck was a duplicated of his, only in a different color.

"Where's my baby?" Sage questioned. The brand new car seat that she saw strapped into the back made her laugh. Lorde was determined that she was Pryce's mother.

"She's at Ora's." That was her nanny, his mother's best friend. "I have something that I want to talk to you about, too." He revealed. "Can we go upstairs and talk?"

"Na, nigga. Nothing has changed. You are still banned from up there."

"Girl, if you don't get your ass out and go tell them people that you made a horrible mistake and you want this good dick at random so they need to take me off the list then I'm going to hurt you!"

"Come on crazy ass dude. For some reason, I believe you."

"You'd better. I don't say shit that I don't mean."

"Come on, Lorde."

Sage slammed her truck door, and pulled Lorde towards her apartment. On the way upstairs, she was sure to let the front desk know that he was no longer banned from coming to see her, and that he could come up any time that he liked.

The second Sage hit the door, her back was slammed against the wall. Her clothes were stripped from her body, and she was hoisted into the air. Relieved that she had shaved a few mornings ago, she allowed Lorde to have his way.

"I've missed you!" he admitted before licking across her swollen nub. "You missed me?" he questioned. "Or did you miss this dick?"

"Both." Her body started to react to the movement of his tongue.

With each flick, she twitched. Lorde feasted off her sweet nectar as she rotated her hands around his bald head. He was going for broke on her pussy, claiming it as if it was his last meal. He continuously dipped his tongue in and out of her opening, causing her to cry out, and beg for more. The way his thick warm tongue caressed her folds, Sage was wishing that he would never put her down.

Those wishes were quickly disbanded when he caused her to orgasm just before dropping her down onto his hard. Sage was in a frenzy as he worked her body over. Their lips met, and he transferred the juices that she'd allowed to spill from his mouth to hers.

"I'm cumming." She yelled, grabbing ahold of Lorde's back. He leaned in, and bit down on her neck, attempting to suppress his own urge to release.

After the shaking ceased, on Sage's end, Lorde pulled himself from her piping hot insides, and grabbed her long ponytail. Forcing her to her knees, he demanding some top.

"Lick that shit off." He whispered in a sultry, yet aggressive, manner.

Sage prepared herself, opening her mouth wide enough to accommodate his large growth. The taste of her remnants caused her to use her own fingers to meddle in her gushy. From down below, she stroked her clit while working her neck to please her man.

"Shit." Lorde used the wall to support his weight. Sage was making it difficult to keep his balance. She blew him away when she practiced skill by relaxing her throat and pushing his dick beyond the back of her neck. He was, nearly, balls deep in her mouth. When she pulled him back, a thick glob of spit hung from her mouth to his piece. That sight did it for him. Before Sage could protest, he yanked her up, and bent her over. His dick was slippery from her sloppy top, and her pussy was just as saturated.

"Fuck." Sage yelled out when he slid in.

Back and forward, Lorde put on a fucking show as he dabbled in the goods. He had a hand full of hair, wrapped around his knuckles, as he gave her back shots. He didn't slow down or lose his rhythm until his dick was spitting up inside of her pretty little pussy.

"I love you." The words fell from his mouth as he emptied himself.

"I love you, too."

An hour passed before the couple was back up from a power nap. They joined one another in the shower for another round, and then got dressed, again. Sage had changed her outfit, opting for some jeans, heels, and a distressed tee.

"So, what was it that you had to talk to me about?" Sage questioned.

"I had my lawyer to draw up the papers."

"What papers?"

"You said to try to get Gia to sign over her rights, right?"

"Yea. Have you mentioned it, yet?"

"Na, but I don't need to. She hasn't called to check up on Pryce since the day we took her from her. She doesn't want anything to do with my baby, and I couldn't be happier."

"Exactly. Pryce doesn't need anyone like that in her life."

"Same shit I'm thinking, but it's going to come at a price."

"Of course!" Sage rolled her eyes. "She's going to ask for something. I can feel it."

"I've got that covered, though. We're meeting her in a few hours. I had to chase her down. The bitch done got her number changed and some more shit."

"Wow. That's crazy. how much do you think that she's going to want?"

"Probably a half a mil."

"You've got to be shitting me."

"She knows I'll pay it." Lorde shrugged.

"I need to stop by my crib before we head to meet her. You ready?"

"Yeah. I'm driving, though." Sage was ready to push her new whip.

"I figured you'd say that. I'll just give you turn for turn directions. It's all good, yo."

"Okay, let me grab my purse, and then I'll be good to go."

"Bet."

**

"She's over an hour late." Sage noted as she continued to eat her backed chicken, macaroni, and loaded mashed potatoes.

"It's all good. When we're done we can jet." Lorde shrugged.

"Yes. I want to see my boo thang and shoot by the mall." Sage had been promised a date. Lorde was pulling out all the stops, and she was loving every bit of it.

"For what, Sage. You have a closet full of shit."

"It's not new shit." She informed.

"You're just looking for a reason to spend money," Lorde leaned back and went inside of his pocket.

"And you're just looking for a reason to give me more, but don't bother. You're coming with us."

"So, you just going to tell me what the hell my day is going to look like."

"You said you were taking the day off to be with us, so I figured we may as well make the best of it." Sage smirked.

"You ain't slick." Lorde mushed her in the side of her face, "but aight. It's y'all day. I'm just along for the ride."

"Good."

As the word left Sage's lips, Gia strutted up to their table with the longest grey weave Sage had ever seen. She wore a pair of jeans, Jordans, and a cropped top. One wouldn't be able to tell that she'd had a child less than three months prior. Sage had to admit that she looked good, but she was far from it. All of that beauty that she sported on the outside did nothing for the ugliness that she embodied within.

"Really Lorde?" Gia asked.

"Sit the fuck down." Lorde didn't give two shits how she felt about Sage's presence.

"What could you have possibly wanted, today?" Gia asked, taking a seat across from Lorde and Sage. They were stationed in the back of the restaurant at a booth.

Lorde pointed at the table where the papers sat. They had been placed where she could reach them. Flipping them around, Gia read over the contents. A sigh followed her brief overview of the paperwork.

"And how do you suppose you're going to care for a child, Lorde?" Gia questioned. "I hope you don't think that you're about to be around too much longer, because in a few months… he'll be on to the next." Gia turned her attention towards Sage.

"Let me worry about that." Sage was unbothered as she spoke, still eating her food.

"Gia. What we talking?"

"What you mean, Lorde? I'm not signing this shit so that you can run off with my daughter and build a false ass family structure based on a lie."

"Every hoe has her price. Name it."

Gia hadn't considered the benefits of this deal that Lorde was proposing. At the mention of money, her eyes glistened. She calculated a few digits in her head before spitting out the first thing that came to mind. "Twenty-five Gs."

"Done." Lorde looked over at Sage with a smirk. This bitch was dumber than he thought she was.

"Now, and twenty-five more after I sign." She saw how easy that was, and thought that she should probably have asked for more.

"Gia, what you think this is? You asked for twenty-five Gs to sign your rights over, and that's what your hoe ass is getting."

"Fifty stacks, and you can have her."

"You acting like you want her any fucking way." Lorde shrugged. "But aight."

He leaned over and whispered into Sage's ear. Lorde, then, slid out of the booth, and allowed her to do the same. Once she was outside of the booth, she exited the restaurant. Lorde slid back inside, and begin his tongue lashing.

"You a pathetic ass bitch. You put up not once ounce of fight to keep your daughter. Even before now, you haven't expressed any concerns for her wellbeing. You asked for twenty-five lousy stacks, when I was willing to pay a mil if that's what you had requested. You're so fucking worried about my bitch, when my bitch is more of a mother to Pryce than you'll ever be. In fact, my bitch is that best thing that could've ever happened to Pryce. When I'm out on the block, risking my fucking life and laying sucker on their asses, it's my bitch that is home caring for Pryce like she's her fucking mother. When Pryce is sick, you know who I call? Huh? When I need rest, you know who the fuck I call? When Pryce needs something… clothes, diapers, milk… anything… You know who goes to get that shit before I can even notice? When I fuck up, and she ain't fucking with me… You know who she's still going to the ends of earth to care for? Huh? You know who a nigga going to wife, and replace you name with on that fucking birth certificate? …MY BITCH. So stop worrying about the wrong motherfucker. What you need to be doing is thanking that woman, because she doesn't have to do none of the shit that she's doing. She's filling in when she doesn't even have to. Not only is she seeing after my daughter, but she's keeping this dick warm, too. Those are two things you can't do even if I shoved a fucking incubator up that pussy of yours, BITCH!"

Just as Lorde finished his last statement, Sage reappeared. She didn't bother sliding in the booth. She handed Gia a pen from her purse, and stood beside her with a paper bag in hand. Gia cut her eyes towards Sage before focusing on the document in front of her. After a few seconds, she signed, and slammed the pen down on the table.

"Satisfied."

"More than you'll ever know." Lorde replied, sarcastically.

Sage snatched the papers up before stuffing them into her purse. She handed Gia the paper bag, and stepped aside so that she could remove herself from their presence. Sage had remained respectful until Gia decided to play dirty with her words.

"I know you think you've gotten over with this measly fifty stacks, but I always get the last laugh." She tugged at her long tresses. "You just paid for fucking baby that doesn't share the same blood with you or anyone that's in your fucking family." Gia threw her head back in laughter.

Before she could bring her antics to a close, Sage was on her ass. She reached back, and socked soul to Gia's face. Her nose bled, instantly, but Sage kept at it. Those pretty grey locks were wrapped around Sage's hand as she banged Gia's head on the table that she'd just gotten up from.

Lorde continued to eat his dinner, chest burning and eyes stinging. He was well aware of the fact that Pryce wasn't his biological daughter, but he'd never voiced the fact outwardly. To hear someone torture him with his reality made him feel diminished inside. His heart was aching, and he knew that if he reacted, he would leave Gia leaking in the restaurant. There was no doubt in his mind that he'd send her to her maker.

He watched as his sweet thang put them paws on Gia. She didn't stand a chance as Sage got down on her knees, giving Gia pure face shots. The owner of the restaurant ran to the back where the commotion was going on, attempting to break the commotion up. Lorde felt as if Sage had a hell of a lot more ass kicking to do, so there wasn't a motherfucker alive that could break that shit up.

Lorde was quick on his toes, pulling his pistol from his waist, and pointing it in the man's face. "I motherfucking dare you to touch her." he yelled. The business owner held his hands up, and surrendered. "She just signed her rights over to her child. She deserves that ass whooping."

Focusing back on his dinner, Lorde polished his plate. "That's enough baby." He told Sage as he wiped the remains from the corners of his mouth. "Aye, homie. Run me them motherfucking tapes." He waved his gun at the owner, and the two begin to walk away.

Lorde followed him to their office, and demanded footage for the entire day. Within a matter of minutes, he and Sage were back in her truck, and off into traffic. He's taken the wheel while Sage fumed in the passenger seat. She was an emotional wreck as she called Gia everything but a child of God.

"Here," she reached into her oversized designer bag, and handed Lorde the paper bag that she'd brought inside of the restaurant.

"Bullshit." Lorde's eyes went from the road to the bag, and then back again.

"That bitch didn't deserve a dime." Sage fumed. "I can't believe she would do something so foul. Like, how do you make someone believe that a child is theirs the entire…"

"Sage." Lorde stopped her.

"No Lorde. That was just not right. And then, she waited…"

"Sage."

"What?"

"I've known that Pryce wasn't mine since before she was born. But it ain't shit nobody on this motherfucking planet can tell me differently." Lorde choked up. "That's my baby girl." Tears poured from his eyes, breaking Sage's emotions down to pieces. She, too, begin to cry.

“When I look at my baby, I don’t see none of that shit. That’s all me right there. You don’t have to share the same blood to be family. I’m daddy. I’m the only daddy that she’ll every know.” Lorde confessed. “I’m the only one that she’ll ever need.”

“That’s all that matters.” Sage cried.

“That shit you heard back there… That shit never happened, aight. Never. Don’t even do me dirty like that bitch and let that slip from you lips. Besides her and I, you’re the only person that knows that. My mother had an idea, but she’s gone.”

“I could never.”

“Good.” Lorde wiped his eyes with his shoulder. “We’re going to get our baby girl.”

Chapter Thirteen

Vacation had done their relationship some good. Now back at home, the two were inseparable. The smoldering hot atmosphere resulted in beads of sweat dropping from SaeKu's chocolate canvas. Her lower lip was tucked between her top and bottom teeth as her back arched and toes curled. Dade's tongue was even more magical than his wand.

"Ahhh." SaeKu cried out to the heaven. "Ummmmm." Her body convulsed, shaking uncontrollably. "Don't stop." She begged.

Dade followed her command, sucking on her inflated bulb while bringing her to a mind-blowing, spine tingling orgasm. He was near eruption at the site of her silhouette, as her body heaved due to satisfaction of his works.

"Shit… Shit… Shit…" SaeKu cussed.

Wanting to experience the fruits of his labor, Dade lifted himself, and reinserted his growing into SaeKu's crevice. Her hands flew to his back, brushing it with her finger tips.

"Yes." She confessed. "Yes."

Harshly, Dade stroked her wet wet, until he found that state of oblivion. Waddling in between reality and imagination, he never wanted to come from within between the two. SaeKu's loving was just too good to be true. Everything was so perfect. Her small whimpers, loud whispers, back arching, tight spaces, slippery slope, and aggression were all pieces to the most powerful sexual encounter that Dade had ever experienced.

Grabbing ahold of her neck, he leaned in and bit into her flesh. He desperately needed to relieve the build up that was slowly approaching, but he wasn't ready. Pulling out of SaeKu, he whispered in her ear. "Come ride this dick."

With that, SaeKu was on her knees in a flash, waiting for Dade to get comfortable. The small time lapse spared him more time. He was good, now, and ready for more. He watched through the dark as SaeKu position each leg beside him, and hovered over his body.

She then reached back, feeling for his erection. Her search wasn't long. It was nearly impossible to miss the swollen vessel that awaited her. Aligning her entrance, SaeKu slid down on the lengthy tool. Her moans told her story of prominent satisfaction for the hundredth time since the commencement of their sexual union.

Up and down, she rode his member until neither could hold back. Dade grabbed her by the waist, taking complete control as he hammered away at her small frame. "It's coming." Dade warned. "Ah. Shit. Baby. Here it comes."

SaeKu tried removing herself from it's path, but it was of no use. Unfortunately, Dade had a hold on her, so she couldn't move. He continued to bounce her up and down as he let loose. SaeKu came along with him, tired and out of breath.

"Come shower." Dade patted her ass, and got out of bed. Once SaeKu could find her footing, she followed Dade into the bathroom. The two washed each other up, went for round two, and was back in bed within the hour.

As SaeKu dozed, Dade's phone buzzed for the third time. He'd been ignoring the caller for the last few hours, hoping that they'd get the point. Unfortunately, they weren't letting up. Lifting himself from SaeKu's embrace, Dade snatched his cell from the night stand.

Alani's name lit up on the screen, signaling that she was calling, again. Looking down at SaeKu, he struggled with the thought of leaving her in bed to go answer, or letting the call roll over to voicemail.

Forty-five minutes later, and his phone was still buzzing. Figuring SaeKu was good and sleep, Dade crept out of bed, and tiptoed down the hall. The minute his ear connected with the phone, he heard screaming and crying from Alani.

"Dade. It's time."

"I'm on my way."

Dade back peddled into the bedroom to grab a tee shirt and some slippers. He snatched his wallet off of the nightstand, and was downstairs in no time. While shutting the door behind him, he was careful not to make too much noise. Dade hopped in his car, and sped out of the driveway. Before he knew it, he was parking his whip and running up to labor and delivery.

**

Dade sat inside of his vehicle, tears threatening to spill from his eyes. With his right hand, he quickly wiped them away. His heart was heavy, and there wasn't but one person on earth who could lift the load. However, he doubted that she would be able to aid him. For, she too, would be attempting to aid her very own wounds –ones that he had burdened her with.

A few minutes passed before Dade was ready to meet his fate. He dragged himself from the car, and into his home. As he walked to his bedroom, he mentally collected every aspect of SaeKu's presence. His home felt so much better with her there. Now, he'd be subjected to the ice cold palace without his Queen to keep it warm.

Upon entering his bedroom, Dade was quiet as a mouse stealing crumbs from a homeowner. He crept into the large space, and made himself comfortable in the ash grey velvet chair that he loved so much. It sat beside his bed, giving him a damn near magical experience. He watched SaeKu sleep, from the comfort of his sofa chair, wishing that he didn't have to be the barrier of bad news.

The sun rose before Dade had realized he had drifted away for hours. His eyes became heavy with guilt as SaeKu began to stir in bed. Before her eyes opened, she felt for him on the opposite side of her. The gesture warmed Dade's heart. When she didn't feel him near, her eyes popped open. As expected, he was near –staring back at her.

"SaeKu." Dade started.

He was gentle with his words, trying to chose them precisely. He'd practiced his speech throughout the night and morning, in his head, but now that his leading lady was awake he could not fathom speaking the words that would rock her world.

“Dade, no.” SaeKu’s face crumbled, and her hands flew to her mouth. The defeat was evident in Dade’s mannerism. It didn’t take a rocket science to figure out what he was about to shed. SaeKu couldn’t bare to hear the words fall from his lips. Her body shook as she lifted her right hand to stop Dade’s commentary before it could even commence.

“SaeKu.” He called out, his voice low and sympathetic. His words were laced with pain. “Just listen…” he tried with her, but that was all that he had left to say. His words were held back, and his thoughts were absent.

“She’s yours?” SaeKu couldn’t stop her lips from moving. “She’s yours isn’t she?” Using every bit of strength that she hadn’t been drained of, SaeKu lifted herself in bed. “Say it.” She demanded.

“SaeKu.” Dade reached out, but was rejected. SaeKu snatched her arm from his reach.

“Just say it, Dade.” She repeated. “Tell me this shit to my face, so that you can see just how much this shit hurts. Go ahead Dade. You deserve nothing more than to see the look on my face when you recite those earth shattering words. Go ahead.” SaeKu begged. “Just say it.”

“She’s mine.” Dade dropped his head, unable to witness the crumbling of such a marvelous soul.

In that moment, he wished that he’d kept everything one-hundred with SaeKu. Knowing her, she would’ve understood. But there wasn’t much time to waddle in regret. The minute the words left Dade’s mouth, SaeKu was out of bed. Her slim body slithered across the floor. The two had made passionate love well into the night, so she was without clothing. Her tresses swung from side to side as she beat the ground with her feet.

"You come into my life like you're going to make everything alright, and you make more of a mess of it than it already was."

"SaeKu." Dade jumped up from his seat, and started behind her. "Please. I'm fucked up behind this shit, too?"

"Really? Do you feel like someone just blindside you, knocking you to the ground, jugging your body with a knife, carving your shit out, reaching their filthy hands inside, and pulling out your most valuable organ? Huh? Is that how you feel, Dade, because that's how I feel." SaeKu cried. Dade went to reach for her, but she smacked his hand away. "I hate what you've done to me." she admitted. "I trusted you."

"You still can." Dade started.

"I wanted you to be different. I wanted you to be everything that I had imagined you would be. I wanted you to be my fucking hero, Dade." SaeKu busied herself by putting on clothing. She didn't bother reaching for luggage or any extra articles. Whatever was at his place could stay. Everything could easily be replaced, much easier than her sanity. With each second that she stayed in Dade's presence, she was losing a bit more than that.

"Stop. Just stop. You're driving me up the wall, SaeKu. Let me talk to you!"

"No. When I gave you the chance to talk to me, you chose the cowardly route. You chose to omit the truth."

"SaeKu, I want to tell you everything. Just listen."

"I don't have time, Dade."

"Make time!"

“Fuck you!” SaeKu could no longer keep her balance. She had one foot inside of her pajamas, and the other on the floor. Before she knew it, she fallen. Not even bothering to pick herself back up, she laid on her back and released her frustrations. Dade’s back slid down the wall of their closet, until his butt made contact with the floor.

“It was one time.” Dade took the time to explain.

“One time. I was on some other shit, and I had forgotten protection. I waved off all caution, and still went with the flow. Honestly, I wasn’t expecting to take things that far. She’d just broken up with her boyfriend, and they were still involved in some ways. The entire time, I was thinking that they had created a child together, but I had my doubts. I didn’t voice them, but I wish I had. Fast forward to me running into you. I was willing to leave out some key details in order to assure your spot in my life. I just wanted you around. I crept out of our bed, last night. Alani called and told me that she was in active labor. When I got there, she was already pushing. After the doctors cleaned her up, at first glance, I knew that baby girl was mine. She has my birthmark, it’s on her ribcage just like mine. We named her Daicee.” Dade choked up at the thought of his daughter.

“She’s beautiful, baby. SaeKu, I know this is a hard pill to swallow, but I am asking you to consider it. I haven’t been anything other than who you’ve grown to love since the day we met. I feel like we’ve been through too much to let this tear down our walls. If you can find it in your heart to forgive me, then please do so. If I have to suffer or wait it out, then I’ll do that. Just tell me something.”

“I can’t be here.” SaeKu was a ball of emotions as she listened.

"Where do you want to go? If you need time away, then that's fine." Dade was willing to take any answer over no.

"No. I can't be here." There it was. She'd said it. SaeKu pointed between the two of them. "I can't come between your happiness, Dade. I would never even want to."

"What are you talking about? You are my happiness."

"I was. I was before this thing. I'm sorry, but I can't go on pretending. I can't act like this is okay, or like I am accepting of the things that you've done. I'm not. The thought of someone having your child tears me to pieces. I had all of these hopes for us."

SaeKu covered her face, and paused for a second. She had to get, both, her emotions and thoughts in line. The two were all over the place. She didn't know if she was sinking or floating, but neither felt good.

"This messes it all up. I can't bare the sight of you kissing and caressing a child that I didn't carry and birth into the world. I can't begin to wrap my head around the thought of me sharing you with your daughter's mother, because that's what would happen. I don't think I'll ever be able to handle late night store runs and weekend visits. I just can't do it. You're asking too much of me." SaeKu was upfront and honest. She'd, already, considered these things beforehand. With the paternity of the baby being proven, SaeKu knew that she couldn't stay.

"I have to get out of here." SaeKu sat on the floor and placed her other leg into her pajamas.

"Don't go." Dade begged.

"I have to. Look at us, Dade. I can't stand the sight of you." Her words tore a hole through his chest.

"SaeKu, I'm not asking you to stay for a lifetime. I'm just asking you to stay for the day. Please." Dade begged.

"This hurts so bad." She huffed, cradling herself with her knees up to her chest.

"I know. I know." Dade scooted closer to SaeKu. "I fucked this all up." He wiped her tears. "And as much as it hurts a nigga to say this shit, I understand where you're coming from. Everything that you said, I get it."

"Why did this happen?" SaeKu questioned. "Why couldn't you just be perfect?"

"Nobody's perfect, baby." Dade scooted closer to SaeKu, wrapping his arms around her. "I'm sorry that you have to go through this. I'm sorry." He confessed. "Please, my conscious can't bare the thought of not knowing you're okay. Just stay the day, and you can leave first thing in the morning."

"You're asking a lot from me."

"I know, but I have to. If you're going to pull your presence from my life, indefinitely, I just want a few more moments. That's all I'm asking… begging." Dade corrected himself. "I don't think you understand what your absence is going to do to a nigga."

SaeKu remained quiet, whimpering in silence. Dade, too, became lost in his thoughts. He was mourning the lost of a profound love. It was as if the universe was combatting their connection at all costs. He couldn't imagine living without SaeKu any longer than he had to, but that was something he'd learn to do.

"You deserve better."

"I deserved honesty."

"And so much more." Dade ran his hand through his curly top. Stress was eating away at his glow. His eyes had darkened, and his chest burned from agony.

**

Puckering her lips, SaeKu landed a kiss on Dade's. He stirred in his sleep, stomach clenching at the thought of a new day. A new beginning meant an unhappy ending for him. The time that he'd spent with SaeKu the day before was heartwarming to say the least. Even in her condition, she tried to make the best of the time that they had left, together.

SaeKu pulled on her big girl panties, and assisted Dade as he went out and prepared for his baby girl's presence. He didn't own a single article of baby gear. SaeKu was an angel as they cruised through the stores, pouring everything that he'd need into their carts. SaeKu had even purchased Daicee a special bag with her name printed on it. She'd given Dade the task of picking it up once it was completed, because she'd be long gone by then.

"Don't go." Dade pleaded.

"We talked about this." SaeKu stressed. "Don't do this to me." She tried getting her emotions in check.

"I'm sorry. I know it may not mean much, but I'm sorry."

"It's okay." SaeKu hushed Dade with another kiss to the lips.

His groans resurrected her emotional outburst as she gave into her very own cries. It pained her to hear a man so strong and mighty whimper like a child hungry for it's mother's breast. With her right hand, she wiped the tears that slid from his lids. Grabbing a hold to her hand, Dade held it to his face before kissing it over and over again.

"I'm sorry." He repeated. "Tell me you forgive me." Dade looked into SaeKu's eyes.

"I forgive you." She admitted. "I was searching for the moment that I'd begin to hate you, yesterday. I waited for the feeling of resentment to cross my mind, but I got nothing. If I have to sacrifice a love like ours for the beautiful blessing that was born on yesterday, then so be it."

"You're like a dream." Dade couldn't understand how God could create a creature so flawless. Selfless in her ways, she still chose someone else's happiness over her own. He'd ripped her heart to shreds, and only hours later she was looking him in the eyes as she returned the favor.

"I'm going to go, now." SaeKu sighed. "I'll lock up behind me. Your key will be under the mat."

"You're returning the key, too?" Dade hadn't rationalized, yet. Now, everything was hitting him at once. He'd put the thought of her leaving out of his mind, hoping that she'd change her mind.

"It's not mine to have, anymore." SaeKu lifted up, and straightened out her tee shirt. She'd gotten dressed, and packed up while Dade slept.

"I want you to keep it."

"I want a lot of things, Dade?"

“Does any of them include me, because we can make that happen.” Dade lifted from his bed. He stretched, and then pulled SaeKu in for a hug. She never answered his question, which he was expecting. “I’m going to miss you.”

SaeKu didn’t respond, afraid that she’d admit that she’d contemplated staying –saving them both the heartache. She was afraid that she’d give into his pleas, and accept the lies that he’d told. She was afraid that she was willing to be whatever he needed her to be in order to make this thing work. She was afraid that she would settle for something that she was not comfortable with. She was afraid that she’d place her concerns on the backburner just to make sure that he was happy in the end.

“Give me one second.” Dade ran into the closet, and then reappeared. In his hand, he held a small velvet box. “I’d bought it the day that I returned to the states. I knew that after seeing you this time, I’d never let go. I was waiting for the right moment to ask, but that moment never came. I’ve been so caught up in my bullshit that I probably even missed it. On our first date, I came close to asking, but I had left the ring back home.” Dade opened the box and pulled the ring out. “But there’s no one else I ever want to put this on. It’s yours.” He handed SaeKu the elegant rock with diamonds glistening. He was certain of her style, so he opt for something less flashy. However, he’d paid much more than a grip for the simple piece. It was laced with diamonds, and the rose gold band had been customized with their initials.

“I can’t take this.”

“You can, and you will.”

“Thanks.”

“Let me help you put it on.” Dade wished that he was sliding the ring onto her finger under different circumstances, but this was it.

“Thanks.” SaeKu marveled over her newest piece of jewelry.

“My pleasure.” Dade nodded. “It’s as beautiful as I imagined it being on your finger.”

“I’ll see you around, Dade.” SaeKu stepped out of his grasp. She needed to get out of dodge before she reconsidered everything.

Turning towards the door, she took one last look at the place she’d grown to call home. As she neared the door, she grabbed the handle of her rose gold suitcase, and tugged at it. The luggage trailed behind her as she made her way through the mini palace. Her tears found their way down her cheeks, again. She’d left her heart at Dade’s feet, and she wondered if he’d even known it. There was no doubt in her mind that this was it. She was done with love. If it wasn’t Dade that she was giving her love to, then it was no one at all.

Chapter Fourteen

Two months later…

Just call him…

SaeKu's mind was playing her, once again. Dade had been heavy on her mind for the last few weeks, but she didn't have the guts to pick up her cell and give him a call. It had been two months since the split, and so much between them had changed. She went from waking up in a mansion and making him breakfast in bed to her small apartment in the Bronx, sleeping past the rise of the morning sun to avoid the memories all together.

The sound of the front door opening startled SaeKu from her thoughts. "Hey." Sage walked inside of the apartment, throwing her keys on the table.

"Hey."

"I'm exhausted, honey. Now this damn boy is talking about heading to Manhattan to do some shopping." Sage complained. "The cold is starting to pick up, and I do not want my baby out there in that wind."

"Didn't you just get her one of those jumper things?"

“Yeah, but it’s not cold enough for that, yet.” Sage was in a funk at the thought of doing anything besides laying around and resting. She’d been gone from her two favorite people for the bulk of the week, and had just gotten off.

“Yeah. That may be a little much.”

“Exactly.”

Things with Sage and Lorde had progressed, tremendously. Fortunately for her, she’d tamed the untamable beast. Sage had him eating out the palm of her hands. After overcoming their difficulties, Sage forced Lorde to date her. His sense of pride had him feeling entitled to her, but Sage quickly broke him down. Just like Sage and Dade, their love story wasn’t conventional, but it was real.

“Forget it. I’ll just bring an extra blanket.”

“You could’ve thought of that first.”

“Well, I did, but Pryce is Pryce. She is busy as ever to be so damn tiny. She’s going to keep pushing that blanket off and trying to play hide and seek and shit.”

SaeKu burst into laughter because she knew Sage was telling the truth. Pryce was five months, but one could never tell. She was spiting out words like Dada and Mama, completely confusing medical providers and overstepping all boundaries set for babies her age.

“That shit isn’t funny. It was you that taught her that.” Sage blamed SaeKu for her troubles.

“Look, we just be having fun.” SaeKu held her hand up in surrender.

The beating at the door made Sage sigh. “This nigga won’t even let me get out of my uniform. Damn!” She huffed, standing to open the door.

"Awwwwww. Aren't y'all just too cute." SaeKu was so happy for her friend. Lorde was a blessing and a curse.

She felt sorry for even little Pryce having to put up with him as a father. Sage had it a bit easier. On the other hand, he'd blessed Sage with a chance at having a family of her own. She'd strayed away from her parents' people, because they just weren't fit. SaeKu had been her only hope for years. Now that Lorde and Pryce were present, they filled the gapping hole that she'd been suffering from since the death of her parents.

"What's up? You ready?" Lorde barged into the apartment with Pryce in his arms. She lit up like a tree on Christmas when she seen SaeKu.

"Damn, can I wash my ass first. I just walked in the door. I told you I would be over in a minute."

"Well, it's been a minute. It's been a few." Lorde leaned down, and placed Pryce on the floor.

"There go tee tee's baby. Come on." SaeKu was determined to teach Pryce to crawl, but she wasn't having it. She scooted a bit, and then gave up. "Little lazy girl." SaeKu laughed, and snatched her up. "I missed you!" she oozed, kissing all over Pryce's stomach, making her laugh.

"Lorde. You get on my nerves like half the time. You act like you couldn't wait until I came through."

"I couldn't. Now what?" he stepped into Sage's personal space. "I really fell through because Pryce be cock blocking and shit. We can fuck right now, and gone get it over with. You have an in home babysitter. Today is the sitter's off day, so that's a no on my end."

"Excuse me." SaeKu looked up from the floor.

"Please forgive this man. He has no filter, Lord. Just work on this fool." Sage closed her eyes, and lifted her hand towards the sky. "Be a fix, Jesus."

Chuckling, Lorde grabbed her hand, squeezing it. He lead her to the bedroom with a smirk on his face.

"Hold up. I need to use the bathroom."

"Well, I'll be right here. Gone and jump in the shower while you're at it, because you ain't bout to sit on my face with that pissy pussy."

"Really?" Sage held her hands up.

"God have mercy on your soul." SaeKu shouted out, shaking her head while laughing.

It was no secret that Lorde said whatever came to mind. He held nothing inside. Around him, you were sure to get a laugh, sometimes a cry. He was just that damn unpredictable.

As Lorde waited on Sage to emerge from the bathroom, he used the time to return Dade's call. He'd hit him up while on the way up, but he couldn't answer due to Pryce squirming all over the place.

"What's good, yo?" Dade answered.

"Nigga, you called me. What's up?"

"I just slid through your crib, and you weren't there. I wanted to get at you about some shit."

"Aight. I'll be settled in a few hours. I'm over at Sage's crib right now. After we hit Manhattan, we coming that way."

"Bet."

"I'll hit you back when we get in."

"Do that."

"One." Lorde was about to hang up the phone when he heard Dade call out.

"Is she there?"

"Yeah." Lorde shook his head as if Dade could see him.

"She aight?"

"Nigga, who the fuck am I to be checking for your shorty. If I'm not sticking my dick in it, then I'm not worried about if it's even breathing."

"Fuck you!" Dade spat, not know why he even asked Lorde anything.

"Call your girl."

"That ain't my girl."

"Let you tell it." Lorde ended the call, not bothering to listen any further.

Dade reclined his sofa chair, and tucked his arms behind his head. Life without SaeKu was no fun, and settling for someone he wasn't truly in love with wasn't an option. The months spent with Alani were all in vain. Still, after all this time, he felt nothing. The love that he wanted to pour into SaeKu, he'd been dispensing into Alani. However, the minute the real deal came strutting into his life, it all went down the drain.

Dade had wondered why Alani never put up a fight when he broke things off with her. Up until recently, she had left the key details out. Apparently, she'd been preparing herself for the day that he walked out of her life. She was well aware that she was on borrowed time. She expressed that the day that SaeKu walked back into his life, she knew that her time was up.

After suffering in silence for a few weeks, Alani was relieved when Dade was up front and honest about his true feelings and the history behind he and SaeKu. He also promised to be there at the birth of her daughter, in which turned out to be his as well. They'd both known the slight possibility, but neither were banking on it. The odds turned out in Alani's favor, because her ex wanted nothing to do with her daughter –whether it was his or not.

Their daughter Daicee was, now, eight weeks old, and the highlight of both of their lives. Dade wouldn't trade her for anything in the world. However, he wished that her presence didn't push away the woman that he wanted to spend the rest of his days with. If he could only get SaeKu to accept him, flaws and all, then all would be good with him.

Fuck it, I'm going to call her. Dade told himself.

He felt like he didn't have anything to lose. Besides, tomorrow was an important day to him, and he wanted her to accompany him. It would be a long stretch to ask, but he was going to do so anyway.

His finger found her contact faster than he could change his mind. When the ringing stopped, and silence commenced, Dade's heart pumped with glee. She'd picked up, and just like him, she couldn't find the words to say.

They both clung on to the fulfillment felt on either end of the lines. Dade was the first to speak, hesitantly. He was afraid to ruin the moment, but eager to speak so that she wouldn't hang up on him.

"I'm ready to forgive her." he spoke. "Like my mom said before she died... As long as I carry that hatred around in my heart, she will forever control me."

"And she was right." SaeKu encouraged, relieved that Dade was finally coming to terms with the fact that he needed to let go of the pain that his biological mother had caused him. Because for every minute she neglected him, his aunt replaced with sheer love.

"I'm visiting her grave, tomorrow. Would you mind coming with me?"

SaeKu was silent for a minute. Although she wanted to stand strong on her word, she knew that they needed to talk. "I'd love that, Dade."

"Thank you." He rejoiced in the background, figuring this was a step in the right direction. "How does noon sound for you?"

"Noon is perfect. Where?"

"She's next to Lauren."

"Dade." SaeKu couldn't believe what she was hearing. Dade had passed his biological mother's grave without even muttering a word the day of Lauren's funeral.

"I know. I know. I visit. I just didn't feel the need to that day."

"Tomorrow, then."

"Tomorrow."

"See you, then." SaeKu and Dade were both prolonging the call, neither really wanting to hang up.

"Yeah. I guess I'll see you then."

SaeKu pressed the end button, wishing that she had more words and more time. "Tee tee is going to see your uncle Dade, tomorrow." She rubbed Pryce's hair. She'd fallen asleep in SaeKu's arms, while they watched Dora. "Tee tee misses him so so much." SaeKu sighed, laying Pryce on her chest as she rested on the floor. "So much."

**

Just tell him how you feel. Tell him you forgive him. Tell him that you want to make this work. Just say it.

SaeKu was hyping herself up as she drove to the cemetery. All night, she'd envisioned how their meeting would end. Hopefully, it would end with hot chocolate and a plan to rekindle through a course of dinners and dates. SaeKu was being hopeful. After she revealed everything that she needed to, she prayed that everything worked out in her favor.

Dressed to impress, SaeKu wore an off the shoulder sweater that was loose fitted, with a pair of distressed denim, and a pair of brown booties. The cold weather was breaking way, so she'd dressed accordingly. Of course, she'd made it to the cemetery before Dade, being that she was rarely on time –but always early.

She gathered the fresh flowers from her backseat, and started towards the plots. She'd gotten enough to place on Dade's biological mother's grave and his mother's as well. During the short time she'd known Lauren, she knew that she loved her boys with everything in her. It was ashamed to see her go so soon.

SaeKu kneeled down to remove the roses that had tarnished from Lauren's headstone. She, then, replaced them with the bulk that she'd purchased at the flower shop. Using her hands, she picked away at the weeds that were gathering around it.

"A little upkeep, huh?" Dade's voice played like sweet melodies in her ear. With her hand over her head to block out the sun, SaeKu looked up at him.

Her heart split four different ways at the sight of him holding his precious baby girl in his arms. Lowering her head, she tossed the weeds into the small bag that held the flowers before. SaeKu lifted herself from the ground, and dusted off her bottom. She hated him for looking so damn good.

"Yeah. Somewhat."

"How have you been?"

"I've been better." SaeKu admitted. "Taking things a day at a time, you know."

"Yeah. I know." He nodded.

"So this is Daicee." SaeKu marveled over the tiny being that Dade held.

"Yes. I wasn't planning to bring her, but her mother called me last minute. That's why I was running a little behind."

"Oh okay." SaeKu nodded in understanding.

What she had hoped to be a magical reunion had gone astray. The words that she'd recited in her head over and over had flown out of the window. The feelings that she was expecting to come from this heart warming meeting had seemingly taken the backseat.

"So, forgiveness, huh?"

"Yeah. It's time."

"It is Dade, and I'm so proud of you for taking this step. I'm sure it would mean the world to your mother. Both of them."

"You're probably right, SaeKu."

"Here. I got these for you." She handed Dade the flowers. "I wanted you to be the one to place them."

"Thanks. I had plans to stop, but that didn't go so well. I didn't want to keep getting her in and out of the car and shit. Having a kid is no joke. I swear this shit gets harder by the day." Dade started on a small rant. "Especially being in two different households and all." *If it's not with you*, he wanted to say. "I'm done. This little girl is it for me." He finished off his statement.

"I have a little running around to do." SaeKu smiled, hiding the pain behind his statement. "I just wanted to be here for you. Ya know."

"I appreciate it." Dade kneeled, and placed the flowers at his mother's grave. "I know this is asking a lot, but I was wondering if you could offer some forgiveness, too. "Dade stood back up, and walked a bit closer to SaeKu. "You know, on my end."

"Dade."

"I'm thinking you, me, and Daicee could make some shit work. Lorde and Sage have a nice little set up going on. It just makes me think…"

"Dade."

"Just hear me out. This is life, and we only have one. Why waste it with pointlessness? You and I both know that we belong together. I'm not forcing your hand, but I'm just stating facts. She's here, SaeKu. She's here, and she's not going anywhere. Yet and still, what does her being here have to do with you and I?" Dade wanted to know. "Tell me, because I can't seem to come up with a good enough answer."

"You wouldn't understand."

"Make me!" he demanded.

"Dade, it's complicated. I guess that she's just proof of how fucked up I really was. I ran for years from something I still can't seem to escape. It's not her. Don't ever think that it's her. It's me, Dade. Me. Even the sight of you with her today pained me worst then the day you revealed that she was yours. This has nothing to do with forgiveness, because I have forgiven you."

"Then what is it about?"

"Acceptance. I just don't have that to give." SaeKu stood on her tippy toes, and planted a kiss on Dade's cheek. Spinning on her heels, she turned toward the direction that she'd come in.

One shot to the chest, and SaeKu was void of life. Dade had killed her very existence. As she treaded the grassy cemetery grounds, her tears cascaded down her beautiful brown cheeks and meshed with the soil that covered the deceased. Empty of life, she felt as if she may as well cop a squat beside one of the tarnished headstones. Because although there was breath in her body, she was lifeless, benumbed, inert, comatose… dead.

"…. But maybe one day?" Dade yelled out behind her, unaware of just how broken SaeKu was.

His absence had caused more pain than the death of her boyfriend Bret. His absence continuously punctured her lungs, beating down on her chest like a raging bull. If only Dade had known that she found herself crying more than she'd smiled lately. Her regret was on an all time high. SaeKu only wished that she'd been more receptive to his pleas of companionship. Had she known the consequences would be a lifetime of unhappiness, she would've sang his praises and took his last name.

Lifting her head, SaeKu searched for an answer. The words just wouldn't come to her. Nodding her head, instead, she threw her hand up to wave goodbye. Never looking back, SaeKu continued to her car, and got inside. Once there, she shuttered. Her walls came crashing down. She had held her composure for as long as her body would allow.

In the driver seat of her ride, she cried for the dear Lord to save her sinking soul. Nothing in life had ever hurt so bad. More than anything she'd ever prayed for, she prayed that the pain would just subside. It had been over two months, and it hadn't let up in the slightest. Everything on her body hurt. From head to toe, there was an aching so horrid that she wouldn't wish it on her worst enemy.

Thick, salty pain induced tears rolled onto the carpet, shedding the pride that SaeKu had mustered up at the sight of Dade with his precious baby girl. Her chest rose and fell with each weep. Her cries were like deep slow melodies that brought more pain than peace to the heart. It seemed as if no amount of crying had helped cure even an ounce of pain harbored.

SaeKu wondered how such a precious pair could cause so much harm, threatening her womanhood in every way imaginable. Daicee was a doll, and SaeKu could never see her as anything but. However, the cruel things that her existence did to SaeKu was tearing her down.

SaeKu spent ten minutes total in her car, calming her nerves. The entire time, Dade watched from his vehicle, desperately wanting to reach out to her. It didn't take a rocket scientist to know what secrets that vehicle would tell. Blinking black his very own tears, Dade shook his head, thinking about the possibilities that had been chalked up. There wasn't a doubt in his mind that SaeKu was it for him. She was everything that he could have ever imagined in a partner.

The cooing of Daicee knocked him out of his thoughts. Taking a look into the backseat, Dade smiled. Although his journey to fatherhood wasn't conventional, he wouldn't trade his baby girl for the world. Understanding just how difficult her presence was to SaeKu, he shrugged off the thought of them ever being more than they were, now –nothing.

Shoving his selfishness aside, he knew that he had to let her be. Never would he force something so vital on someone. Letting the love of his life find love and happiness elsewhere was the price he was willing to pay, not only for SaeKu, but for himself and his baby girl, as well.

"Or maybe next lifetime…" Dade whispered to himself as he caught the single tear that tried falling. With his shoulder, he cleared the residue. With one last look towards SaeKu's direction, Dade gathered his bearings and pulled out of the cemetery.

Chapter *Fifteen*

"It all falls down..."

"Ms. Noble." The nurse startled SaeKu.

She was lost in her thoughts, contemplating sending the message that she'd been sitting on for the last twenty minutes. Her words were sincere and her thoughts were valid. However, neither could justify the selfishness of her decision. Inwardly, she felt a burning desire to shed light on her situation. But then again, she figured it just wouldn't change things.

Only time could heal broken hearts, and that was just something SaeKu was willing to bank on. Adding to the problem would only double the disappointment, knowing that things wouldn't quite work out the way she'd imagined it for the last few years. In fact, nothing had gone according to her imagination. Even as she sat in the cold and lonely building, preparing to sin in the worst way, she knew that this was not the way that her love story was supposed to be written.

"Uh, yeah." SaeKu looked up.

"You can come back, now."

Gathering her books and other belongings, SaeKu stood from her chair, and followed the nurse behind the thick wood door. Tugging at her sweater, she pulled it tighter around her shoulders. After making it on the other side of the office, she was seated again. SaeKu couldn't understand why they'd called her back from waiting out front, only to wait some more.

Surveying her surroundings, SaeKu noted the dull facial expressions of women gathered around the waiting area. Everyone seemed so detached, to life in general, as they waited to be called next. As her wait begin, again, she slouched slightly in her seat, pulling out, "Thugs and The Women Who Love Them," a story that she'd read over and over again.

An hour passed before SaeKu was called, once more. She'd nearly twirled the ring that Dade had given her from her finger. It had become a habit. Most instances, she didn't even know that she was doing it. This time, she was lead into a room that was furnished with a bed and two machines. "Get undressed from the waist down. There is a gown on the bed for you to cover up your bottom half. I'll be back in a few minutes." The nurse rushed out of the door as fast as she'd come.

SaeKu's nerves started to get the best of her when left alone in the cold room. Chill bumps covered her arms and legs, stating her case. She was scared out of her mind, and somewhat reconsidering her decision. The bright lights were too much to bare, and the mental stress she'd been subjected to made the situation even worst.

"Get it together, SaeKu." She preached to herself, pulling her sweats down.

Lifting back up, she threw them onto the chair near the wall. She caught a glimpse of her reflection, and did a double take. Standing sideways in the mirror, she observed her growing abdomen. She could barely wrap her head around the fact that there was a life growing inside of her. Many nights, she'd dreamt of wedding and baring Dade's children. What she hadn't dreamt of was months of heartache and a lifetime of pain surrounding their seemingly perfect connection.

Staring back at her was evidence of what could have been between she and a man so special and perfectly constructed that she nearly wanted to expurgate her eyes. The what if, maybe, should've, would've, and could've were all present in her mirrored reflection. Turning away, SaeKu climbed on the bed and grabbed her cell.

The nurse waltzed back into the room, and lifted her shirt. "This is going to be cold, so bare with me."

"Okay." SaeKu nodded.

"We're going to get an ultrasound here, to see just how far along you really are."

"Do I have to watch?" SaeKu questioned.

"No ma'am. I can turn the monitor the other way." The nurse sympathized.

"Thanks." SaeKu grabbed her headphones, and plug them into her ears. She didn't want to see or hear the love button as it floated around in it's rightful place. It would be too much for her.

As the nurse went about her duties, curiosity ate away at SaeKu. Reaching upward, she removed one earbud from her ear. The thudding sound of the monitor was soothing. Her pain subsided as she listened on. She wanted to hear more of the music to her soul. She reached over and tugged until the other earbud fell beside her head.

Immediately, emotions overwhelmed her. SaeKu could stop the overflow of tears that gathered at her neck after falling on the sides of her face. Although she'd insisted on not seeing her little nugget, she just couldn't resist. Her voice was low, and shameful as she begged of the nurse's assistance.

"Can…" she could barely form a sentence. "Can you turn it around?" she questioned. She wanted to see. She needed to see.

"Sure sweetie."

And there it was, the only thing that SaeKu had left. Her child was remnants of a love so profound that the earth couldn't even stand it's assembling. She had no clue what she was staring at, but she was both in awe and utter shock. Instantaneously, she was attached to a foreign being that she would soon have to detach herself from. In a matter of minutes, she'd be legs wide stretched, having her little one pulled from her womb, away from it's nest and put to rest. Before it's life could even begin, she was ending it.

"Turn it back around." SaeKu cried. "Please." She could stand no more.

Silence swept the room as she waited for the first portion of the procedure to be over. It was minutes before she was left alone, again. Grabbing her phone, she decided that she would send Dade the message that had been burning her text box to be sent. But before she did so, she revisited her gallery. Under the video tab, she searched for the very first video she'd made of her pregnancy. It was the very day that she found out they were expecting. Opening the video, her chocolate skin appeared on the screen.

"Okay, Dade. So, I've been feeling a little in the dumps lately. I thought that it was a stomach bug, but my cycle has yet to come." SaeKu explained. "Plus, I've been feeling light headed for the last few days…"

SaeKu was going over her symptoms as she sat the phone on the bathroom shelf, where it could record her movements without her holding it. She was shaking like a leaf on a winter evening as she produced the pregnancy test from the Walmart bag.

"... My cravings are just down right stupid, and I haven't felt like doing much of nothing the past few weeks. Basically, I figured this may be something worth looking into." She placed the pregnancy test box in front of the camera. "It took me so long to buy this thing. I've been nervous out of my mind."

SaeKu chuckled, tearing the box open. She read the directions out loud. "Hopefully, I do this right." She laughed. After taking each needed step, SaeKu pulled the toilet seat down, and sat.

"Now, we play the waiting game." She shrugged.

Seconds passed before she begin to talk, again. "I really wish you were here." She admitted. "I really wish this was a moment we were sharing together." SaeKu choked up on her words. "You could set the timer and I could go lose my mind for three minutes while we await the verdict of our future." SaeKu called it exactly how it would've happened. "I love you, Dade." A smile tugged at her cheeks.

The buzzer sounded, letting SaeKu know that the time was up. "I'm going to let you take a peek first. Ready?" she asked.

She then turned the camera around to the countertop, where the test laid. SaeKu, then, looked herself. "OH MY GOD!" she exclaimed. "OH MY GOD! Dade, did you see that? Huh? Did you see that? Look!" she put the camera back on the test. "I'm pregnant. Oh my God. I'm pregnant." She repeated.

Turning the camera back towards her, SaeKu confessed her fears. "I'm so scared right now. How come you aren't here? Oh my God. We're having a baby. We're having a baby." SaeKu covered her mouth, looking around trying to decipher what was reality and what wasn't.

"This is crazy, Dade." She cried. "I don't know what to do with myself." SaeKu was full of fear and joy at the same time. "MUAH." She kissed the screen of the phone. "I'll call you, tonight."

"Ms. Noble." The doctor came in the minute the video ended.

"Yes." SaeKu sat up, wiping her tears.

"I'm Doctor Rolls, and I'll be administering your procedure. I'm going to gather the staff and take care of the patient next door. After that, we will be in."

"Okay." SaeKu nodded.

"See you in a bit." The sweet old lady left the room, leaving SaeKu alone with her thoughts, once again.

It wasn't even a full ten minutes before the doctor was back inside of the room. Her staff lingered behind, preparing for the procedure as she'd promise. In a flash, SaeKu's legs were hoisted into the air. Before her cell was taken from her, she attached the video she'd just viewed to the message that she'd been contemplating about for hours. As the sounds of the irritating machine commenced, SaeKu recalled each word that she'd written in hopes that Dade would understand her decision. Closing her eyes, she became physically numb to the pain, as she repeated the truth that she'd revealed within her message to the love of her life.

Dade,

As I sit in this cold and lonely clinic, I feel as if I owe you the decency of revelation. I'm with child, and you're the father. I'm certain that goes without saying. However, this message isn't to boost your pride, and welcome you to fatherhood –once more. This message is to inform you of a decision that I've made, and you've assisted me in making. Our worlds are so distant and different in every way. It would be selfish of us both to bring a child into the chaotic structure. Let's just consider this a mistake, because neither of us intended on this happening. In my efforts to get you to understand where I am coming from, I want you to know that I understood everything you said about the difficulties of having children while we were at the cemetery. I wish to burden you no more than you've been burdened. As I prepare to have the most heart shattering procedure I've even undergone in my life, I just wanted to wish you well. I pray for forgiveness from you and the man above. I also pray for a life of peace and abundance on your end. I love you. I'm sorry, but I can't have this child.

SaeKu

Instagram: @mercy.b

Facebook: Mercy B Carruthers (Join my group HERE or by going to bit.ly/mercymafia.)

Twitter: MercyandCo

Periscope: MercyandCo

Snapchat: MercyandCo

"Memoirs of A Drug Lord's Wife"

Order HERE.

Prologue

April 2000

The sticky residue of semen trailed Pei's lips as she swallowed the last of the load that had been poured into her throat. Salty and unpleasant to the taste, she could easily distinguish the fact that it wasn't of who she'd desired. Squeezing her eyes closely together, she held back the tears that were threatening to cascade down her perfectly chiseled face.

In just a moment's time, the painful reminder of her reality nearly caused her to gage from the offensive act that she was participating in. Shaking her head, she willed herself to retain the disgusting fluids that she'd just attained. Daring not to look herself in the mirror that sat directly in front of her, Pei refused to acknowledge the distasteful image it was sure to display.

"Shit." She heard his voice, and it nearly caused all of her efforts to be in vain. However, she held it together.

Shortly after, she felt the pickled size penis being removed from her flushed right cheek. It had been resting there since spilling its solution into Pei's mouth. Still on her knees, which were sore from the shagged, rough carpet covered concrete floor of her dingy motel room, Pei remained silent. Slightly relieved that the act had been completed, she found solace in accepting that her John's absence would soon come to fruition.

The clinking of a belt buckle, followed by a zipper told his every move. His feet shuffled as he tried to hurry out of the door, probably returning home to his wife and children. Pei could give a shit. He was the only factor standing between herself and the solitude that she craved.

As the door frame of the motel connected with the door, Pei breathed. Finally opening her eyes, she used the emerald colored rounds to stare at the tarnished image before her. From the pit of her stomach, Pei bellowed a blood grueling scream.

Barely recognizing her reflection, she yanked the deep burgundy wig from her skull, and her short blonde waves appeared. After tossing it to the left of her, Pei used her right hand and smear the already ruined eyeliner that traced her cheeks. Anguish tugged at her once rehabbed heart, causing her to pull at her face –screaming once again. Digging her nails deep into her skin, Pei cried out for something, anything.

She was confused as to how her life had spiraled so rapidly. From sugar to shit, she'd been apart of a sick whirlwind –ending in tragedy. Her skin burned as the tears filled the scratches she'd placed on her skin, feeling like pure acid poured directly on to her face. The physical pain that she felt was nothing compared to the broken spirit she was suffering from, so she didn't bother to acknowledge it.

Falling back onto the heels of her feet, Pei's ample ass kept her sitting fairly high. Her unblemished high yellow skin scalded, much like a pot of boiling water, as her back heaved. More than the act that she'd just committed, she cried for it's reasoning. She'd never felt so hopeless in all of her years.

After the numbness in her legs gained control, Pei had no other choice but to raise from her seated position. Still in shambles, she stared down at the single bills sprawled over the tattered carpet. A darkened idea surfaced, causing Pei to consider a time when a manmade substance used to remove the thought of her misfortunes –even much of the pain at times.

Closing her eyes, she tried disowning her own thoughts for a split second. Just as soon as her eyes opened again, she lost the battle. The dampened thought returned, pegging at Pei. Blowing out in frustration, she fought the mental battle tooth and nail. She'd been brought from that place, and promised to never return.

Feeling filthy, Pei looked down at her one-piece ensemble. She's refused to remove it. Even in her desperation, she remained mindful of the ultimate that she'd partake in had she allowed anyone in her most treasured possession. Oral pleasure was deemed less rebuking, so it was much painless than the other.

A shower was necessary, immediately. Grabbing the White Diamond body wash from the chipped night stand on the side of the bed, Pei headed towards the bathroom. Holding the cool bottle against the flustered, revealed skin on her upper chest, Pei savored the moment. The bottle of pleasantry reminded her of the times.

Fortunately, she hadn't always been cooped up in a low budget motel, sucking dick, and drinking cum from strangers pickled sized penis'. Even though there were times, before her saving, that were drastic, they had never gotten so merciless. Quickly clearing her thoughts, Pei reminded herself that the past was just that. In order to survive her day to day hardships, her mind must be null of it –facing only the tasks set before her each day.

Reaching the bathroom, Pei cringed at the stained walls. One would be moved by the broken mirror over the small sink, but Pei was appreciative of it. The less she faced her reflection, the further she could run from her reality. Picking the single towel from the rack, Pei placed it on the counter before pushing the tan colored shower curtain back to start the water.

Seconds passed before the bathroom became engrossed in the steam emitting from the steaming hot shower. As blistering as the droplets felt on her bare skin, Pei withstood the searing pain that was of consequence. She felt her filthiest, so the sizzle was necessary.

Tears, just as thick as the pellets attacking her skin, meshed with the water –unnoticeable. In the moment, Pei felt as helpless as newborn fresh from it's mother's wound –prematurely birthed. Grabbing the shower curtain, she tried to break her fall as her knees weakened under her. Life as she knew it was gone, and replaced with one not worth living any longer. On the floor of the rusted bath tub, Pei allowed the steaming water to cataract down on her curly blonde mane. Head in hands, she was overcome by grief.

Pei's showered proved to be more difficult than she'd anticipated. Hoping to be cleansed as she soaked, she was everything but. Sure that the older pipe smoking couple that was just next door could hear her sobs, Pei paid the thought no mind. She was exhausted. It was all exhausting.

There hadn't been a time that she could remember things being so difficult. The water went cold as it continued to beat down on her palpitating back. Up and down, it continued to maneuver, evidence of hollowing cries. Collecting herself, only after a full hour, Pei found the strength to raise from the floor of the discolored bath.

The demons returned, riding her back as she placed on the soiled robe that hung from the bathroom closet. Fighting was much harder than giving in. Being that her soul was weakened, even in a two-hour time period, Pei allowed her demons to storm her being –crowding her out. Licking her dry lips, she swallowed an air bubble as she began to crave. The familiar itch caused a very distinct twinge on the barrier of her skin.

Darting her eyes over to the money that she'd just been given, the wheels in Pei's head began to turn. Bending over, she wiped her legs dry with the towel that she'd placed on the counter prior to showering. Lifting back up, she was faced with the broken mirror above the sink. Although it was completely in shambles, it still revealed her fire engine red eyes, puffy lids, and flushed cheeks. Right there, there it was. The most horrific sight. Reality was gazing back at Pei as she soaked it all in.

"This can't be life." She begged the differ. "It just can't be." Her naturally horse voice sounded bruised, along with her pride and ego.

Touching her face, Pei just needed to be sure that she wasn't trapped in a tragic nightmare. Her scolding hot skin assured her that this was it. This was real. Twisting her lips into a frown, she bore a look of repugnance. Turning from the mirror, she stormed out of the crammed restroom, striking her smallest toe on the end of the bathroom door.

Yelping in pain, she fell face first into the carpet, that reeked of dried cum, condoms, hot pussy, and outdated chips. Using her hands to push herself up, Pei commenced to grabbing each dollar that was in sight. Crawling around on the thick, prickly carpet, she collected her funds. Her tears collided with the remnants of the already filthy floor.

Depleted, Pei grabbed a big t shirt from her small plastic bag. Continuing to dig, she found a pair of dingy black tights, with fur balls in the crotch area, and stepped inside of them. She searched for her wig, and threw it on her head before grabbing her coin purse. Stuffing the money inside of the lime green chained tote, she hauled ass –sure to take the small key card that she'd need to get back inside.

"HEY! You!" Pei heard just as she stepped out of her motel room door. The place was barely standing. Hustlers, hoes, pimps, and con artist were all spread out amongst the parking lot. A variety of occupants kept the establishment afloat.

"HEY!" She heard again, but she kept striding. The hotel owner had been on her case for nearly a week. It was the reason she tried to avoid the likes of him each day.

As bad as Pei needed the money that she'd just made to pay for her motel stay, she needed a release even more. She didn't care that she was three days late on her bill, and the owner was threatening to throw her out on her ass. Nothing more mattered than the task at hand.

"GET BACK HERE!" He yelled as Pei continued on the opposite end of the motel parking lot.

Glancing over at the badly built motel owner, Jimmy, Pei saw that he was headed her way. Picking up her speed, she got a move on. She didn't want to risk him taking the money that she'd just earned. With the type of heart that she had, she'd give in and give what he was due. However, tonight, she desperately needed each dollar. There was no way she could afford to pay him at the moment.

Jimmy's belly jiggled as he made his way across the parking lot, disregarding the cars that were sounding their horns as he cut in front of them. Pei's heart began to race as she tried to clear it. Her thrift store bought ashy white, high top Nike sneakers tore away at the ground as she made way. The closer Jimmy got to her, the faster she walked –eventually turning into a light jog. With each step that she took, the pieces left of her broken heart shattered onto the splintered concrete.

"I'm sorry," Pei yelled as she reached the door of the yellow cabbed that she'd spotted when she first stepped out of her door. She really wasn't a bad person, not at all. Life just had its way of ruining even the most beautiful souls. Unfortunately, she'd fallen victim to its wrath. "I'll have it for you in the morning!"

Placing her hands on the back of the cab, she used it to stop her stride. Breathing hard, she turned back to see Jimmy stop where he was. Throwing his hands in the air, he didn't bother pursuing her any longer. "Ahhh!" His heavy Italian accent was notable.

"Promise!" Pei yelled back as she yanked the cab door open. Hopping inside, she breathed a sigh of relief, and rested her head on the seat.

"Where?" the driver asked.

"West 123rd." Pei spoke.

"Okay."

"Wait. Just drop me at Amsterdam."

"Got it." The older gentleman spoke. His broken English caused Pei to cringe. The foreign cabbies could barely drive.

The ride to the Manhattan high rise was silent. Besides the heat and radio tunes, nothing more could be heard. Pei stared out the window as they passed the streets of New York. Just a few months ago, everything looked so different. Maybe not technically, but in her eyes everything was much different. In the short time that her life had spiraled, she viewed everything differently. Taking note of the city's life, passing her by, Pei wondered what more she had to live for. Her complete world had been snatched from her, within a day's time.

Dropping her head, she thought over everything that ever meant anything to her. Nothing was more profound than the love that she'd received. Now, it was all gone. Emptiness filled the gaping hole that kept her from being whole again. Pei felt as if she was just being kept alive out of spite. Finally, her pass transgressions were catching up to her, and she couldn't stand it any longer.

As the cab came to a stop in front of the project housing, Pei braced herself before opening her door. She couldn't help but to question her moves. Wondering if she really wanted to take herself back down that lonely road again, Pei tried to decide before allowing the cab driver to pull off. She'd nearly gotten back in the car, but the smile on the fiend's face as he shot pass the sidewalk that she was standing near changed her mind. Just like him, she wanted something to help her locate smile. It had been lost for months. Before slamming the cab door, she reached in and handed him the amount that he'd quoted to her upon their arrival.

"Thank you!" she used her manners.

"Safe." The cab driver warned, looking up at the courtyard of the projects. It looked more like a huge cemetery.

Disregarding his remarks, Pei shut the door and turned to face the night. Checking her surroundings, she stalked up to the familiar grounds. She'd trekked them under different circumstance. Hoping that she was undetected, Pei pulled her wig down on her head even more. She didn't want anyone recognizing her. Bad news spread faster than the good, and she didn't want to be the talk of the town. Pei had moved to an entirely different burrow just to avoid being the source of criticism in Manhattan.

The dark of the night caused Pei to be much more alert than she'd had to been in some time. Her keen senses kicked in as she listened attentively. She could hear everything from the crickets to grasshoppers chirping. She didn't understand where they were hiding, because the yard lacked healthy grass. The scarce patches were nowhere to hide. After what felt like eternity, Pei finally made it to the designated area. Pulling her money out of her hand, she walked up to the tall, slender figure that was pacing. Every few seconds he'd look up.

Everything about him was the same. Pei remembered Shy, and everything about him. How could she ever forget him? They had shared so many different spaces together. At a point, they were both on a pedestal. The same even that sent her crashing, sent him tumbling as well.

From the looks of everything, Shy seemed to be bouncing back. He was looking like old money as Pei approached.

Disguising her voice, she called out a number. “Fifty.”

“Here you go, shorty.” A quick exchange, hand in hand, rewarded Pei with the product that she desperately needed. “Get yourself somewhere safe. The jects ain’t the idea place for young lady like yourself.”

Shy had always been very caring. Even the harshness of his dilemmas couldn’t turn that man cold, and Pei loved him for that. He was just a stand up dude, always creating positivity in the most negative of situations.

“Thanks Sh…” Pei caught herself before she finished her statement. Holding her hands over her mouth, she turned and tried to speed off. She had what she’d come for, and needed to get the hell out of dodge. Without a doubt in her mind, she knew that he’d heard slip of the tongue.

“Ayo?” he whispered, loudly. “Pei?” he asked just before she cut out. She was quickly caught up to. Feeling her arm being snatched backwards, Pei was spun around to face Shy once again. He almost didn’t recognize her with the burgundy wig. She’d lost a bit of weight since they’d last seen one another, but she was still a nice size. The wear and tear on her face proved that her life had been a bit less than pleasant. Shy’s heart immediately went out to her.

“What’s good? I’ve been looking all over for you!” And he wasn’t lying. He and Willow had searched the city, but didn’t find a trace on her.

Lowering her head, Pei's mouth began to water as she held the sack of dope in her hand. She was anxious to get back to her motel to intake as much as her body would allow. The night would be one to remember.

"Yo, why you buggin?" Shy asked, lifting Pei's hand –the one that contained the heroine that she'd just purchased from him.

"Stop it. Don't do that. Don't judge me." Pei shook her head, not feeling the least bit shamed. At least she had an excuse. Life, that was her excuse. It had beaten her down.

"You shitting on my mans right now, and you yappin about me not judging you? You clowning, Pei. Don't do him dirty like that!"

"Don't you dare go there." Pei yanked her hand away and pointed in Shy's face. "How could you even?"

"This ain't the answer." Shy shook his head. "Let me help you."

"I can help myself!" She chastised.

Had Pei heard those words hours ago, before sucking dick and feeling sorry for herself, she would've allowed Shy to do as he pleased. However, with the heroine in her hand, all bets went out of the window. She wanted nothing more than to feel the sting in her veins as the potent drug cruised through her body –taking her far away from her problems.

"Don't do that, shorty!" His heavy New York accent tore away at Pei as she stood, conflicted. "You're better than that." He pointed to her hand.

"He left me SHY!" Pei gritted, frowning her face at the painful memories that flooded her mind at once. "What the hell did he expect me to do?"

"Live shorty!" Shy spoke as if she'd asked the dumbest question known to man. "And this ain't no way to do it."

"Fuck you!" Pei threw up a finger sign before turning and walking off.

"How can I live, Shy? He was my fucking life." She threw over her shoulder before she had gotten too far.

"Shit happens, yo, and then life goes on!" Shy yelled back.

Pei didn't bother to turn around and stare into his pretty skin. Shy was a slim guy, standing at 6'6 in height. He had dreams of becoming a ball player, but the streets grabbed a hold of him before the court could claim his heart. His love for the streets grew as the years passed. When it was time for his peers to go off to college, it was the furthest thing from his mind. By then, he was the sole provider for his mother and siblings. Taking the responsibility as the man of the house, Shy grinded day in and day out.

Back in the shagged motel room, Pei slammed her back against the wall and fell to the floor. She'd been out gathering supplies for more than an hour. She was feigning so badly that she couldn't take another step. Like yesterday, she needed her pain to dissipate. The encounter with Shy had put her on edge, flooding her with grief. He'd completely demolished her with his words, digging a bigger hole in her fragmented heart.

Dumping the contents of her lime colored purse, Pei leaned forward while scrambling to find the things she'd need. The big round silver spoon was shiny, even in the dimly lit room. Grabbing the elastic hair band next, Pei stretched it out until the threads broke, and it tore apart. It now resembled a rope, string, or black cord.

Unfortunately, Pei had to borrow a needle from Drew, the infamous heroine abuser that lived at the motel just doors down. She prayed that it was as sterile as he claimed it to be, because at the moment she had no plans to double check. Clipping the back of her lighter, she was sure to get the most fire out of it so that her block could burn swiftly.

Grabbing the medium sized piece of heroine from the bag, Pei placed it onto the silver spoon. Noticing that there was a broken piece or two left in the bag, she emptied them onto the spoon as well. She was to leave nothing behind. Fed up with the life that she was leading, Pei wanted nothing more than to end it. Right there, on the motel room floor, she wanted to end it all.

Flickering the lighter, she held it against the spoon. Her eyes glistened as she caught wind of the familiar smell of cooked dope. Once upon of time, she felt as if there was nothing better than that aroma. That was before he'd saved her. Blowing out in frustration at the thought of him, Pei caused the fire of the lighter to alter, shifting in the opposite directing.

Pei's patience grew thin as the piece of heroine melted. Finally, the foul smelling drug had changed states. Now a liquid, Pei quickly removed the lighter and grabbed the needle with the attached syringe. Placing it on the spoon, she suctioned the liquid into it's tube. She filled it nearly to capacity.

Her body was full of glee as she thought about the venture she would go on once she was injected. Sitting the spoon to the side, Pei hurried and grabbed the hair band that she had broken. Circling it around her arm, she crossed each end and pulled tight, creating one knot just above the crease in the middle of her arm –on the opposite side of her elbow. Her light skin made it easy to find a vein worth stabbing. Tabbing her arm, she set her sights on the most visible green line that she could find. They were all screaming out at her, but she chose the most aggressive one. It was popping right out of her skin.

Grabbing the needle, Pei pushed the back of it until a tad bit of the liquid oozed out. She didn't want to catch any air bubbles, so she tapped the needle with her index finder to get rid of them. Once satisfied, Pei aimed for the vein that had been begging for her attention.

"Ssssss." She winced once the needle penetrated her skin.

She was able to hit the vein on one try. Realizing she was in the perfect spot, Pei watched as she pushed the tail end of the needle down, shooting the liquid into her vein. She had the right mind to stop once she was nearly halfway in, but couldn't. The little voice in the back of her head persuaded her to continue pushing. And so she did, until she'd emptied the needle's contents into her system.

Immediate relief sat in. A calm like never before smoothed over Pei as she removed the hair band and needle from her arm. Standing to her feet, she staggered over to the thin mattress that sat on a set of rails and threw herself on to the bed. Numbness consumed her as she smiled. She hadn't felt this good in months. Not since life gave her its ass to kiss. Not since she'd been forced to whether the storm. Not since her trials and tribulations became more frequent than her times of joy. Not since Naimeed, her drug of choice.

"Naimeed," she heard herself call out. There he was, once again, saving her. Only this time, he was at the end of the lighted path beckoning for her as she stood under a dark cloud. His pearly white teeth shined as he waved her over –only she couldn't move. Stagnant, she tried reaching out to him, but her body lacked the strength.

Tears rolled onto the already soiled mattress as Pei found herself crying once again. This time, they were tears of joy. Staring back at him, she silently thanked him for the life that he'd awarded her with. In that moment, she wasn't the least bit upset with his abrupt departure. With her eyes closed, flashbacks of the times she remembered the most became vivid. The money, the cars, the traveling, the house, the hood fame, and the love were all right there.

"Pei," she heard him call out, some time later, as the memories began to fade, slowly.

Still smiling, she visited her pass as if it were a movie. Memories, they were all apart of the game. In the end, they were all some had to hold on to. In Pei's case, she felt as if they were enough. As her body began to shut down, vital organs failed, and her brain began to disengage, the memories continued. Even in her final moments she wore a smile, as she recollected on her past, in which produced the memoirs… ***Memoirs of a Drug Lord's Wife.***

Please be sure to review...

CPSIA information can be obtained
at www.ICGtesting.com
Printed in the USA
LVOW10s2122100417
530296LV00015B/663/P